Tom

Christie Moore

authorHOUSE®

AuthorHouse™ UK Ltd.
500 Avebury Boulevard
Central Milton Keynes, MK9 2BE
www.authorhouse.co.uk
Phone: 08001974150

Published by AuthorHouse 1/4/2012

ISBN: 978-1-4678-8072-5 (sc)
ISBN: 978-1-4678-8073-2 (e)

Thanks to:

My Mum and Auntie for the stories about my
Grandfather

My Auntie Brenda for proofreading the story

My brother Mike whose courage to fight cancer is so
much like the character of Tom

Charlotte of Varlet Farm for sharing some of her infinite
knowledge of WW1

the staff at the Postal Heritage Museum at the back of
Mount Pleasant sorting office

the staff at the National Archives of Kew

CHAPTER 1

A POSTMAN'S THE LIFE FOR ME

IT IS THE SUMMER OF 1914; a lone figure is walking along a street in Kilburn, West London. He is tall, wiry and full of joy; He walks upright and never looks down. He walks with briskness like the summer morning, wearing a smart uniform and carrying a large bag. The bag is full of letters; he is a postman delivering this mornings mail. He is Thomas Lane, people call him Tom.

Tom likes his job as he gets to meet people, and he especially likes the dogs. His work colleagues are scared of them as the dogs like to chase postmen, but Tom keeps chocolate in his pocket for when he comes across such animals. They growl at him but he inches forward slowly with a bit of the chocolate in his hand and offers it to the dog. It takes the chocolate and eats it, then be friendly towards Tom. No other postman in the area has this knack of dealing with dogs.

After giving the dog a friendly pat on the head, he walks down the road in the early summer morning as people begin to appear on their way to work. Tom always gives them a cheery 'good morning' whether he has a letter for them or not. Despite his happy appearance, it is opposite to the area he is working in; the houses have been here for over forty years as part of the creeping urbanisation of the London countryside. The streets are narrow and the houses three stories tall, giving the area a closed in feeling, and there is much poverty here. But this doesn't deter Tom who just tries to make everything seem better than they actually are.

He is accosted by a man who has just appeared at his front door.

"Morning Tom" says the man "letters for me?"

"Ooh yes, you have a few....here"

"Have you heard, Germany is preparing for war"

"Oh I don't think so, they wouldn't dare risk war" says Tom trying to be his usual optimistic self.

"Honest" replies the man. "They're building up their armies, and that Austrian chap got himself killed"

"Well" says Tom, "it's a sunny day and we're here aren't we?"

"S'pose" replies the man who is starting to be infected by Tom's cheeriness. He goes off on his way to work with his letter and a slightly springier step. Tom continues on his way holding his next letter while he gets the address of the envelope, his next destination.

Tom finishes his round and walks along the Grand Union canal on his way back to the Kilburn sorting office. He sits down by the bank, eats a piece of his chocolate and drifts off in the warm weather. He thinks back to 1904 when he was a boy and taken to an exhibition down at the Crystal Palace in Sydenham. The size of the place, it is the biggest greenhouse he'd ever seen. He walks through the entrance into this massive lit up cavern filled with interesting stuff, he wasn't aware though that this exhibition was nothing like the original one in 1851 to which Grandpa William went to. But he doesn't care as there are steam engines, petrol engines, cars and all sorts of mechanical wonders. He thinks then that when he grows up, he will own a motor car. He walks for what seems like miles along a vast tunnel of glass, past the boring electric cookers. Mother is interested in those, not that she can afford one. He remembers vividly the full sized model village street exhibit with house fronts and model people inside the houses. A sign in the street says "the Germans are invading". Marching down this make shift road is a group of German soldiers, at the head of this group is the Kaiser. They have their distinctive helmets on, with a single spike coming out of the top of the helmet. Their boots make a heavy sound as they march down the street, then come to a noisy halt as the soldiers stamp their feet.

Tom is both scared and fascinated. How can this be? German soldiers here inside this building, in this country? What Tom doesn't know is that the soldiers are just actors dressed up as German soldiers. It s an illusion to get people thinking about the prospect of a German invasion. And it worked for many boys like Tom.

The man dressed as the Kaiser bends down and asks Tom "vot is your name, little boy?"

Before Tom can speak, a British soldier appears "don't tell him son"

Tom gasps as he looks up at the Tommie dressed in his khaki's. Behind him are a few more British soldiers.

"You start talking young man, and the German soldiers will get information from you without you even knowing"

"Ya, ve vill" says the Kaiser

"We'll see off the Germans, won't we lad?"

Tom stammers "ye-es s-sir"

The Tommie stands with his rifle and asks the German soldiers to leave. The Kaiser looks angry, goes red in the face but turns and orders his men to retreat.

The Tommie leans forward again and puts his finger to his mouth "ssh, keep information to yourself", he rubs Tom's hair

Tom runs off to find his parents.

He then drifts back and says to himself "ha, they were only actors"

He drifts back to his remembrance to later on, still a boy and playing here on the banks of the canal with his friends. Tom tells them of the exhibition his parents took him to and they would talk about the Germans invading the country and how they will stop them single handedly. They'd lie in wait behind the tall grasses and then jump out in front of the canal boat man. "Pow", "pow", "pow" they all shout as they mimic the noise of a gun. Then Tom and his friends say to the boatman as he holds onto to his horse "you're the Kaiser and you're now dead".

"Ar! So you lads will stop the Germans invading will you?" he said

The reply came back "yes we will, you wait and see" as they all run off into the tall grass.

Tom slowly comes back to reality and looks up. It is the boatman he has just thought about, and he is guiding his horse down the towpath.

"Hello sir" says Tom "I was just thinking about you"

"Oh how's that?" says the boatman

"Well, we used to jump out on you when we were young boys and pretend you were a German"

"Oh yes, I remember. You still going to kill Germans then?"

"No, I don't think they'll invade"

With that Tom jumps up with his sack and walks away

"Bye then mister boatman"

"Bye Tom" he replies

"Oh I didn't know he knew my name" thinks Tom.

With that he continues walking back along the canal to the sorting office.

The Kilburn sorting office is at number 258 Belsize Road, just off the Kilburn High Road. The traffic is busy today, the usual horse and carts, but also some motor cars. He weaves his way across the crowded road; this is one of the main arterial routes in and out of London. The postman's entrance is round the back but Tom is at the front so he walks through the main doors, why walk all the way round? The front door leads to a room where there is another door, through which he walks. There is an enormous room and racks of letter holes line both sides, with a gap down the middle. As he walks down this gap with his empty sack, people are milling around sorting letters.

"Afternoon Tom" comes a cheery greeting.

Tom replies back with the same cheeriness he's received and all the way to the back of the hall is this greeting repeated from various people. This same routine is carried out every day, it is due to Tom's infectious happiness that spread like a disease, but this disease makes people feel better. Near the end of the hallway, the room turns to the left where there is another large space at the end is some lockers where Tom leaves his sack.

On the wall, Tom sees a poster urging postmen to join the reserve army, the Post Office Rifles. They had fought during the Boer War and now Tom wants to join. While he stands looking, a fellow postal worker joins him.

"You going to join Tom?" asks William Harvey.

"I might Bill" replies Tom, "yes, I will".

At that moment, Tom Lane marches straight to the postmasters' office. Printed on the door is Sydney Walters Postmaster, he knocks and enters.

"I'd like to join the Post Office Rifles, Mister Walters sir" he says.

"Oh, very admirable" says the Postmaster as he opens a drawer and pulls out a form "I was in the Boer war myself, you know"

"Yes sir"

"Just fill this in and hand it back to me, I'll send it off for you".

Later in the evening, Tom is enjoying quiet drink at his local, the Falcon. He says to his Postal colleague "I've joined the Post Office Rifles"

Bill replies "what did you do that for?"

"Oh, I don't know" says Tom "it seemed like a good idea, you know, adventure, going places and firing a gun"

Bill says as he's about to sup his drink "I might join too then"

At that moment, another chap accosts Tom.

"Here Tom, give us a tune"

"Alright, I will"

And with that he moves lithely to the piano, lifts up the cover and starts playing. The chap who asked Tom to play is standing by the piano with his elbow on the top of the instrument, with his beer in his free hand; then he starts to sing, with other people gradually joining in. Tom plays all night until one in the morning and then walks home. He has a lot of alcohol in him but he is one of those people who doesn't lose control of his bodily functions. He doesn't stagger but walks briskly; anyone looking at him will not know he is drunk unless there was a closer inspection. He is walking down Malvern Road, home is a minute's walk from the pub, and he is at his front door, number 118. He quietly slips his key into the lock and turns, click it goes and he slowly opens the door and creeps upstairs. He reaches the first floor and just about to put his foot on the first step of the stairs to the next floor.

"TOM! IS THAT YOU?" comes a loud woman's' voice, it is his mother.

He turns and she is standing at the door of her bedroom and he says to her "good day to you mother".

"Don't you mother me" she replies "you've been down the pub drinking again; it's all over your breath".

"I only had one...or two maybe..."

"You should be in bed instead of gallivanting around in the middle of the night"

Another voice from inside the bedroom, this time his father "leave him be Ada, he'll suffer when he gets up for work later on"

With that, mother disappears inside the bedroom and closes the door. Tom just stands like a naughty schoolboy who has just been told off. He mutters to himself "oh well" and carries on where he left off, that is creeping up the stairs.

But Tom does get up for work and apparently without ill effect. Some of his colleagues were at the pub last night and are complaining bitterly of foul heads with queasy stomachs.

"What's the matter with you lot, anyone would think you had a good time?" says Tom.

"Please, don't speak so loud" comes the reply from Bill.

He laughs and picks up his sack and off on his round.

Tom plays very well on the piano; he is also in a big band and has a gig that night. Once he finishes his round, he goes straight home; it is around four o'clock in the afternoon. This is the advantage of having a job that starts early; he can finish early and pursue a hobby like music. His mother looks at him with disdain.

"You got this show tonight?" she says to her son as he sits down at the kitchen table. He replies "ooh yes, a grand affair too, at the Hammersmith Town Hall".

"Tch" says his mother "I suppose you'll be out late tonight as well. You need to settle down young lad"

The show is due to start with a large audience packed into a fair sized venue, the band play all the popular numbers of the day. With these gigs, Tom earns a small supplement to his Postal wages. He stands in backstage waiting to go on with his band. Nobody speaks to each other; they are psyching themselves up for the gig. Tom, as happy a chap he is, gets nervous before a show. Everyone does, it is well known in the business, lose the nerves and it's time to give up, it's that apprehension that prepares the soul for the best performance. The compere walks onto stage and adjusts his dickie bow.

"Ladies and Gentlemen, please raise your glasses and welcome for your entertainment, the POSTAL MINSTRELS"

It's time to go on. The band members walk to their instruments on the stage to loud applause. Tom walks to the piano; also in the band are a trombone, big bass, banjo and drums. The audience slow down their clapping to near silence, just the odd cough here and there, waiting in anticipation. The band starts to play, and play they do all evening to an enthralled audience, men raise their beer glasses in appreciation. At the end of the show there is a standing ovation and Tom and the band all take a bow before going off stage.

The next day at the sorting office Frank Bushnell, a colleague asks how the gig went.

"Great Frank" says Tom "a full house"

"You still good with those dogs"

"Oh yes, lovely things. Cheer my day right up they do"

"I don't know how you do it, they just chase me away" he says, "well what are you doing tonight?"

"Well, I hadn't anything planned."

"Good, come down to my local and we'll have a drink"

He walks down to Kensington to the pub where he meets his colleague at The Golden Cross in Lancaster Road.

"Aaah Tom, over here" says Frank as he walks through the entrance.

"That's me brother Ralph over there" he moves closer to Tom "he works here you know"

Tom joins in with a knowing smile. Frank turns to a handsome young woman and says "this is my sister Ellen"

"Hello"

She replies "hello"

The little group get chatting when somebody says "I hear Tom that you play the piano"

"A bit, and occasionally the banjo too"

"Well, there's a piano sitting idly over there"

"Yeah Tom, play for us"

The little group get rowdier as they try to convince him to play but he eventually gives in and saunters over to the piano. Almost immediately a crowd gather round to join in with the sing song. His face lights up as half-pints of beer start to appear along the top of the piano. He turns to look at Ellen and she smiles sweetly at him.

The end of the evening and people say their goodbyes, Tom puts on his jacket and asks Ellen if he can see her again to which she replies that she will.

"Come and meet my family" she says

"Alright, when, where?" asks Tom

"5 Basing Road. It's quite close to here. Tomorrow night"

And with that, she joins her brother and leaves the pub.

Tom is excited the whole day that he has a date tonight, he walks back into the sorting office quicker than normal but no one notices anything unusual as Tom is a happy person anyway. He goes to his cubby hole to see if there are any company notices or letters for him, nothing.

Tom washes well that afternoon and makes sure he has a close shave. He comes downstairs where the whole family was sitting in the kitchen. Father had just come home. His name is Thomas too and he is a decorator. Next to him are Toms' sisters, Liz and Ada. Cousin William is also sitting at the table as he lives there, he is also a postman. Also at the table is Toms' uncle Albert who is staying for tea tonight. Liz asks him "how's Grandfather?"

Albert replies "oh, he's fine. He seems quite content".

Everyone knows Gran'pa William isn't totally happy, his wife died nine years ago and he has never been the same.

Tom manages to butt into the conversation "hello everyone. I'm sorry but I'm not staying for tea this evening. I'm going out"

Liz turns to Ada and quietly says "Tom's got a date" and with this they give a quick giggle.

Mother says in her usual Victorian manner "I suppose you'll be out late tonight"

Father looks up and says "leave the lad alone, this is his chance for him to settle down. You want that don't you?"

Mother says nothing but she has the look on her face as if she wants to say something else, another little dig at Toms' night time drinking habits perhaps.

"What's her name?" enquires Albert

"Ellen" says Tom, and with that he put his jacket on, says his goodbyes and walks out. There are calls of "good luck" and "have fun" as he opens the front door. As he closes the door he smiles to himself.

He walks down Malvern Road to the five star junction with Shirland Road, he takes Waltern Road which leads down to the Harrow Road, a main highway out of London; it is a wider road but still, nonetheless, closed in by tall buildings. He crosses over being careful not to trip over the tramway rails, and walks down to Great Western Road. This takes him over the canal where he often walks, and finally down into the Borough of Kensington. The whole journey takes less than half an hour, hard going by most people's standards. But Tom is not most people; he is a postman and tramps miles everyday. This journey is nothing to him.

He gets to Basing Road and stands there surveying the street. "Number five" he mutters to himself. He stands there holding a bunch of flowers and some chocolate that he had picked up on the way, wondering if he had done right to bring them. Finally, he looks at the door with the number five on it and walks to it. The area seemed more upmarket than he was used to, even though he has seen better places than this on his rounds, he feels a slight apprehension.

"This is worse than going on stage" he thinks to himself. Still, he is not one to back down from many situations. He knocks on the door and a middle aged woman answers.

"Hello" she says, and before Tom can say anything she says "you must be Tom, come on in"

"Thank you, you're very kind".

She takes the flowers and leads Tom into the dining room. Ellen is seated at the table, along with Frank and Ralph, the pub man.

"Hello" says Tom; his nervousness disappears at seeing familiar faces.

"Is your father not joining us?"

"Sorry Tom" says Frank "but Father died years ago"

"Sorry" says Tom

Ralph pipes up "how was your show the other night?"

"Great" says Tom and he relays the events of the evening which kicks off the conversation for the evening as the food is being brought in. Most of the conversation is set around the Post Office; Tom tells the small party that he enjoys being a postman (to which Frank nodded in agreement) because it means he met people.

"Don't forget the dogs" says Frank

"Oh I love the dogs" says Tom

"Dogs?" says Ellen

"Go on Tom, tell everyone how you deal with the dogs" urges Frank

The rest of the evening the small party laughs with Tom and his recollections of his postal rounds and how he feeds dogs with chocolate.

The following day Tom finishes his round and goes through his usual ritual of going down the pub.

"Again?" wails his mother

"We-ll... yes" replies Tom

"Hold on there just one moment young lad" says Tom senior as he stands up with a stern look on his face he wipes his moustache with his fingers,. The two men look at each other for a moment, perhaps father is going to give his son a lecture. Adeline is sure hoping so.

"I'll come down the pub with you, lad" he says much to the disappointment of mother.

He picks up his jacket and father and son walk out. Adeline stands there alone in the empty kitchen as she hears the door slam shut.

Tom and his father walk along Malvern Road towards the Falcon.

"Well son, your mother's got the house to herself" says Tom senior

"Where's Liz and Ada then?"

"Gallivanting with their fellas I think"

"Oh"

Tom senior turns to his son and asks "isn't it about time you did the same? I heard you had a date last night"

"What? I'm far too busy. I don't want to be wasting time with something like that. There's far too many things to do"

His father laughs.

"Never mind" he says "war will be upon us soon"

"Noo" says Tom "I don't know where people get that idea from, it's all propaganda you know"

"Mark my words, my son; the Kaiser will be coming soon"

"Father!"

"It's true. Germany's building up its armies"

They both reach the pub.

"I'll buy" says Tom senior

"That's the first thing this evening that I'm agreeing with you"

The two men sit down with their pints, Tom senior pulls out his watch and looks at the time.

"I had better not stay late otherwise your mother will be upset" he says

Tom looks at the watch "I've been meaning to ask you about that watch"

"Oh yes, this watch, my son" he holds up the timepiece and waves it at his son "was given to me by my father on my twenty first birthday"

"So it's an antique then?"

The expression on fathers faced drops "cheeky! I'm not that old!"

His expression returns to normal "this watch is over twenty years old and still going. Very reliable is this watch" He returns it to his waistcoat pocket.

Before either man can say anything more someone comes over.

"Tom, what are you sitting there for when there's a piano lying idle?"

Tom senior nudges his son "go on Tom, I like to hear you play"

As per usual, he doesn't need much encouragement and quickly walks over to the piano. It is at this moment that his father realises that young Tom is onto a winner as drinks appear on top of the instrument.

The evening finishes, tunes were played, songs were sung. The two men stagger down the road; however, it is Tom who is more in control. Every now and then, he steadies his father as he makes a trip.

"I think you had a few too many father"

"Nonsense, you drank more than me. You wait till you get home, mother will be furious"

Both men laugh. They approach the front door and Tom senior manages after a few attempts to put his key in the door.

"Now then son, make sure you don't do anything that shows you've been drinking"

Tom can't help but smile. The door opens and both walk in, closing the door behind them and creep up the stairs. As they turn at the top stair, they are aware of a figure in the dark.

"Where have you two been? Do you know the time?" says an angry mother

Tom looks at her and smiles "father does, he's got a watch"

"You need to get to bed now" she says.

Tom starts to climb the stairs as his father stands at the door of his bedroom.

"Goodnight son" says Tom senior

"Goodnight father" Tom replies

Adeline has enough; she pushes her husband roughly into the bedroom

"Get in there you drunkard" she says and then slams the door.

Tom is left there at the bottom of the stairs.

"We had a great evening" he says and walks up.

The next day, Tom finishes his round and about to clock out when he is summoned to the Postmasters office.

"Come in Tom" says the Postmaster "sit down".

Tom sits opposite and waits for the man to speak.

"It seems they've accepted you into the Post Office Rifles" he says.

Tom perks up "yes, fantastic isn't it?"

"Now, you get two weeks paid leave for when you are called away but anymore than that and you have to use your holiday. You should get a letter sometime soon. Alright Tom, off you go"

"Thank you Mister Walters".

Tom rushes home and sure enough there is a letter waiting for him, he sits down at the kitchen table and mother asks him what's in the letter.

"It's my admission into the Post Office Rifles. They want me to go to Hayling Island for induction".

All mother can say is "I suppose you'll be with a bunch of lads out drinking"

But Tom isn't listening as he slowly walks out of the kitchen reading his letter. Mother just tuts to herself and within minutes Tom comes back and says "I'm off out, I'll be back later".

"Will you be back for tea?" she calls after him, but Tom doesn't hear as he is already out of the door.

He walks to Basing Road in the warm summers evening and knocks the door. Ellen's mother let him in but before Tom can walk through the door a young girl comes from behind and pushes past Tom, then runs upstairs.

"She's in a bit of a hurry" Tom chuckles then walks in.

"Yes" replies Mrs Bushnell "that's young Ruby. She's the daughter of the Bakers who live upstairs".

She points and a man is standing at the top of the stairs, he is wearing his waistcoat unbuttoned and his shirt sleeves are rolled up, and he is smoking a pipe which projects out from under his moustache.

"Hello Mister Baker" she says

The man pulls the pipe from his mouth and replies back "oh hello Mrs Bushnell, I hope Ruby hasn't been troubling you"

The little girl peers over the railings of the upstairs banister.

"Oh no, she's fine"

Mr Baker turns to the little girl and tells her "come on you little rascal, get inside", and they both disappear into the flat upstairs.

"Bertram is his name, fine chap, a builder you know. Sometimes he does the odd repair for me"

Tom walks down the corridor; Ellen is sitting in the chair in the living room. They look at each other.

"Hello Tom" she says happily.

"I have something to tell you" says Tom

"Oh, nothing terrible I hope" replies Ellen.

"I've joined the Post Office Rifles"

"What's that?"

"It's like the army but we don't fight. We just fire guns and learn….things"

"Tom, you always do the things you want to, I really admire you for that"

"Thank you, but my first event is this weekend at Hayling Island"

CHAPTER 2

THE KAISER'S COMING

THE END OF JULY 1914 and the sun beats down in the mid afternoon summer. Tom has been here for two days out of his five day induction course with Company No.5. He's introduced to his commanding officer Captain Beddy, to his fellow riflemen and a brief course on etiquette and safety. Today he is introduced to the gun, a Lee Enfield rifle and the British army use it. The instructor stands at the front telling the men about the gun, its history, its components and its use. Tom has already dismantled the rifle, examines and puts it back together. He has a sense of pride holding his rifle and throws himself into the maintenance lesson with relish, lapping up the new skills he is learning.

The men are led outside of the wooden hut to the field it stands in. Most of the chaps are from all over the country but Tom knows Messrs Harvey, Kent and English. They are from the same sorting office as him and Tom often drinks down at the local with William Harvey. The men stand in line and point their rifles.

Tom leans his head over "hello Bill"

Bill Harvey replies "fancy seeing you here Tom"

"So, you did join then?"

At the far end of the field is a large grass bank. Tom thinks there are probably hundreds of bullets in that bank. In front of the bank are fresh targets placed for the new recruits.

"Now" says the officer "here is your ammunition"

He hands five bullets to each recruit. Tom, along with the other men, slots each of the bullets into the top.

"Alright, you are going to fire a gun" shouts Captain Beddy "I want you to aim and pull the trigger"

He looks straight at the men and says in a sarcastic tone "and please, keep the bullets in this field"

The men give a muffled laugh at this joke.

"When you are ready, fire at the targets in front of you"

All the guns go off. Most of the targets had been hit, but Tom feels pleased with himself, he is quite sure he has hit the central portion of the target. All the guns fire again, and again. After firing all five bullets each the officer shouts "finished?"

"Right, let's go and see how you did shall we?" he says. All the men lower their weapons and walk with their rifles to the targets, the officer reminds them to keep their rifles in a safe position. The men look at how they've one and were in general pleased with their shooting. Most have hit the targets and a few have got close to the centre but attention is pointing to Tom who stands by his target beaming. The men notice that he has got four out of five bullets through the centre with the fifth close to it.

"It seems" says the officer "that we have in our midst someone with natural shooting talent"

Captain Beddy asks the men to replace their targets and to get back to their firing positions and continue shooting. On the whole, the officer is pleased with the shooting abilities of the whole platoon.

Tom is back at work and has finished his rounds, the other men have gathered round him to listen to his tales of his shooting week. The other three men who are in the Post Office Rifles are there too, but people love to listen to Tom; he has a way of telling an event that has the listener riveted. Although most of the men are excited at hearing of these stories, it doesn't inspire any more of them to join up.

The third day of August brings with it devastating news as Tom walks down the street; the newsboy shouts "Germany invades Belgium." He quickly pulls some coins out of his pocket and hands them over to the newsboy, then walks off with a newspaper.

Back home, he is sitting at the kitchen table with his newspaper wide open. His mother is cooking, and then his father walks in.

"Hello love" he says to his wife then turns to his son "hello Tom"

Tom just carries on reading.

Mother says "he's been reading that newspaper for hours"

"Eh?" Tom sticks his head out from behind his paper "oh hello father"

Father replies "what's so interesting in that journal that you have to ignore us?"

"Germany"

"What?"

"Yes, Germany has invaded Belgium"

"Hmm" says father "the house we've been decorating, the lady there said that. She said that her husband is going to join the army"

Tom carries on reading "oh yeah?"

"Yes my lad. Have you thought of joining up?"

"Nooo" comes a voice from behind the paper

Mother joins in "it'll do you good, make a man of you"

Toms' sisters come in. Liz snatches the newspaper from Tom and puts it to one side,

"It's rude to read at the table" she says

"Ah, hello sis!"

As the two girls sit down, mother puts food on the table.

Liz turns to Tom and asks "so brother, are you going to sign up and be a soldier"

"No need, the Germans won't do anything silly, don't you worry"

Mother pours tea from the pot and with milk added, Tom picks up his cup and "slurp!"

"Aah, there's nothing like a good cup of tea"

"Don't slurp you tea!" says mother

"But mother" he replies and looks straight at her "you make such a lovely cuppa"

Tom is on his way home; he stops and strokes a dog when he hears the newsboy shout "read all about it, Britain at war". He rushes to the news stand and buys a paper. He's transfixed at the headlines and stands on the pavement continuing to read. He folds up the newspaper under his armpit and runs. He gets home and changes before rushing off past the kitchen. Mother sees the blurred figure run past but then Tom comes back and sticks his head in through the doorway.

"No tea for me tonight mother" and then speeds off again.

He walks at a fair pace. Running up the steps to the grand house, he knocks on the door. Ellen's mother opens the door and lets in Tom.

"Ellen…" he says running out of breath.

"Calm down and take it easy, come on, breathe slowly"

"Ellen… we're at war, you know what that means?"

"No, what?"

"I'll probably have to go to France to fight"

"Oh" is all that Ellen could say.

Tom pauses for a bit and then says "Ellen… would you marry me?"

Ellen looks straight into Toms eyes, gives a big smile and says "yes...of course"

It seems that a lot of other people have the same idea as the earliest date they can get is the day after Christmas Day, the only Saturday available. It is a modest affair but it is a large family; Tom and Ellen look lovely as they pose for the cameras. Even mother manages a smile, of sorts. Finally, her boy might grow up and be more responsible. Afterwards at the reception, both Liz and Ada keep asking Tom "are you going to sign up now?"

"Come on girls, I've just got married" as he sips on his beer.

A friend grabs the beer out of his hand and leads him away.

"Forget that Tom" as the man sits him down at the piano "come on play"

The rest of the evening descends into a sing song, which carries on until after many of the guests leave. 'Keep the Home Fires Burning' is everyone's favourite. Finally, Ellen manages to tear Tom away and both go home.

1915

The New Year and it is cold. Tom is still on his round, a bit of bad weather isn't going to put him off one bit. He still has his chocolate in his pocket and is feeding a dog. His hands are a bit cold but he warms them up by sticking them between the letters. But now the dog is relishing the piece of chocolate given to him. As he strokes the dog the owner appears.

Tom looks up and says "lovely German Shepherd"

The owner replies "excuse me, but that is an Alsatian", emphasising the 'that' with a pointed finger.

"Of course" says Tom "we can't have anything German here, can we?"

The owner, a middle aged portly man with red cheeks, then asks "so... are you going to join up then? A young man like you, this country needs fit men like you at the Front"

Tom stumbles with his reply "well, I...er"

"Well, you think about it. You need to do your bit"

The man takes his dog with him as he walks off, leaving Tom standing there, thinking.

Back at the depot, he finds a letter in his pigeon hole quickly tears it open and reads. It's a letter from his superiors at the Post Office urging him to join the army. Every male employee receives one and many men did join up. Tom is unsure, he has heard many men never came back but he does want to do his bit for the war effort.

Many younger men at the office have already gone including Bill, the war hasn't finished as everyone thought. Two of the older men Lionel and Vernon made suggestions to Tom that he should join up when Ralph comes in with a newspaper. He notices the headline and points to the paper under the man's arm, takes a closer look at the newspaper and gasps "they can't do that".

"Can't do what, Tom?" says Ralph

He pulls the newspaper from the man's grasp and reads it.

"The Government have passed a law that pubs are to close at eleven at night. That cuts down on serious drinking time"

He picks up his coat and walks home on this cold February day. There is snow about but all he can think about is the curtailing of his drinking time. He reaches home that he and Ellen have managed to get themselves, their own place a little further down the road to his parents, an apartment at number 96. He has a letter in his pocket which he picked up at the office, he can do that sometimes as he is the mail, it doesn't need to be delivered to his house; but it remains unopened. He sits down at the kitchen table.

"You off down the pub tonight?" says Ellen

"Yes"

"I suppose you'll be back late?"

"No, about eleven"

Ellen is surprised "that's early for you"

Tom turns and looks up at her "the Government have passed a law limiting the opening times of the pubs"

"Oh" says Ellen trying to look concerned but deep down, she is glad. She can have her husband here at home more often. She picks up Tom's coat that was lying over the back of a chair and notices the letter sticking out of the pocket.

"You have an unopened letter there" she says pulling out the letter.

"Oh yes" says Tom as if coming out of a daze. He tears open the envelope and reads the letter.

"It's an invitation for a weeks training in June" he scans the letter "in Fovant, that's in Salisbury"

"Are you joining the regular army?"

"No"

"Do you think you should?"

Tom looks a bit put out "haven't we discussed this?"

"The chap down the road has joined"

March and on his way home from work, Tom decides to visit his parents. He walks in as he normally did but doesn't expect to see his father, who should be at work. But when he walks in, his father is there.

"Oh, it's you Tom" is mother's way of being pleased to see her son. But Tom doesn't reply, he stands at the doorway with shock on his face. There is his father sitting at the table with a mug of tea. He is dressed in the British army uniform.

"Father, what have you done?"

"Well son, I'm in the army now, the Middlesex Regiment, no less"

"Yes... but... but...when did you join?"

Tom senior is very pleased with himself and beams from ear to ear.

"Yesterday, they took me no trouble. Fit as fiddle, they told me"

Tom is still having trouble accepting his father as a soldier.

"But.... you're too old. You're..." Tom thinks for a moment while he calculates his father's age "you're forty seven!"

"I told 'em I was forty. They believed me you know"

Tom slumps into a chair

"Cup of tea?" is all his mother could say

"Aren't you bothered? Don't you think you should be concerned?" Tom asks his mother

"Nothing to do with me" she replies

"Aren't you going to join up then son?" asks Tom senior

"NO" Tom says sternly "look, men don't come back from the Front. They go...and that's where they stay....forever"

Father leans forward "don't be so dramatic"

"It's true! Whole platoons get wiped out. Mother, tell him. You won't come back"

"But I'll die a hero"

"I don't want you to go. I want my father... here" Tom makes a stabbing motion towards the floor with his finger.

"Look son, I'll be alright. They won't send me to the Front; I'll be moving rations and ammunition, stuff like that. I'll probably never see a German"

It is no good, Tom grabs his jacket.

"I'm off down the pub" he declares angrily.

On his way out he slams the front door.

"Hmm" says Tom senior "I don't think he's very happy, Ada"

The thirty first of May Monday morning, Tom and Ellen are asleep in bed but Ellen wakes up to a strange sound. It's a droning sound and she gets up out of bed. She slips on a dressing gown and walks towards the window. Outside in the street a lone policeman on a bicycle is cycling past shouting "get to the shelters" and in the distance are searchlights. Tom appears behind Ellen and asks "what is it?"

"Can you hear that sound?"

"Yes, someone described that sound to me" and with that he rushes off with his dressing gown in his hand to the kitchen window at the back of the house to get a better view.

"Tom?" pleads Ellen, and then follows him.

Tom slips behind the black curtain, pulls up the sash window and puts his head outside looking into the distance.

"What is it?" she slowly puts her head outside too and towards the direction of Toms' gaze, she sees a sight so overpowering. A giant cylindrical monster floating in the sky, its sides flashing bright in the searchlights. This is the source of the droning and it floats gracefully slowly through the night. Below it are flashes of light and fire.

"That..." says Tom "...is a Zeppelin. The Germans are bombing South London"

"Shouldn't we get to a shelter?" asks Ellen with some concern in her voice.

"No" he replies "it's too far away to cause us any damage"

They both continue to watch with fascination at this German killing machine. Suddenly Tom points.

"There, those tiny dots. That's the Royal Flying Corps. That's our boys".

Indeed, the RFC have been alerted and fly up into the night. The guns on the ground had not enough power for its bullets to reach the giant beast. The double winged planes fly towards the huge bag of gas, the pilots look with amazement at the sheer size of the flying machine. The pilots have enough of wonderment, they had a job to do and the leading plane opens fire. The bullets pass straight through the material with no effect on it at all. The pilot makes a pass over the top, quickly followed by the next plane also firing with little effect, followed by a third plane. The planes quickly turn around for another pass. And another firing all the time, during which, the Zeppelin continue to drop its deadly cargo on the innocent civilians below. One pilot gets lucky though, a spark from a bullet ricocheting off the girder structure within, only small but enough to ignite the highly flammable gas inside. The fire spreads slowly across the insides of the gas bags.

Tom and Ellen continue to watch with both horror and fascination to the battle in the air. Tom quickly spots the fire and points saying "they've got it; our boys have hit the Germans". The fire now spread rapidly, engulfing the Zeppelin and very slowly, it starts to sink. It took a long time for the ship to fall and as it does, it becomes a huge fireball. Eventually, the large flame falls into the Thames and by now, several people have gathered at their windows along with Tom and Ellen. A man shouts "yeah and the same to you Mr Kaiser".

Tom turns to Ellen and says with glee "that's a few more dead Germans" and walks back indoors.

Ellen shakes her head and mutters to herself "yes but they are people in that ship too, they have mothers and wives".

CHAPTER 3

PIANO PLAYING PRIVATE

Tom has arrived at Fovant station, a village near Salisbury in Wiltshire. He has been in the Post Office Rifles for a while now and has made the rank of corporal. He disembarks the train and walks down to the village centre with a few other men where they are directed to a field at the foot of the hill. Along the field is a row of wooden huts and the men are sent to their hut. He sorts out his locker before lining up on parade. The day is spent marching and shooting. The evening comes around and Tom goes to the entertainment hut where they have a bar.

"That's more like it!" he says.

But before he can get to the bar he is stopped.

"Tom? Is that you?" it is one of the locals from one of the pubs that he sometimes plays at. He doesn't know the man but many people know him, it turns out that his name is Frank Herbert from Willesden. Before Tom can say anymore the chap says "come on Tom, give us a tune on the piano"

It doesn't take long before the rest of the men (both Rifles and the regular army) get wind of his playing abilities. There is a near riot as men manhandle Tom towards the piano.

"So, you want a tune do you?" he asks.

A cheer goes up with lots of agreements.

"Alright" says Tom as he sweeps his arm across the top of the piano "line them up".

With that, glasses of beer start to appear on top of the piano as he bashes out tune after tune, with soldiers singing along. The party goes on until half ten at night when the order comes for the "lights out in twenty minutes".

Tom slowly stirs from his sleep. Today is Sunday; no drills today just church services. His head swims but there is no headache, his tolerance to alcohol is still there. The rest of the hut is empty, just himself, he must have drunk more than the others as he slept in. He pulls back the sheets and sits on the edge of the bed. Suddenly, the door of the hut burst open, it's Frank.

"Tom, come quick. They're digging in the hills, putting their badges in the side of the hill".

"Who?" Tom replies "who's digging?"

"The other regiments, come-on we've to do our badge as well, grab your shovel".

He gets dressed then finds himself a shovel and marches towards the hill and sees there, in the distance, chalk starting to form in the shape of regimental badges. He quickens his pace and climbs the hill. Once he reaches halfway up his comrades in his regiment have already started to dig and so he quickly joins in. Great clods of grass come up and the chalk underneath is exposed. By the afternoon, the Post Office Rifles regimental badge is complete along with the other badges. At the bottom of the hill are officers watching the day's efforts.

"Hmm, shouldn't those chaps be more productive?"

"By Jove, I couldn't think of anything more productive" replies the other officer "stirs up pride to see those badges, don't you think?"

Tom comes down from the hill, grabs a bite to eat and sits by the road looking at the badges on the hill, feeling proud of his and the other soldiers' achievements. He has been thinking a lot lately, the poster campaigns, the constant nagging from his sisters, mother, wife, his father joining up, the zeppelin and seeing his regiments badge up there on the hill. He thinks now is the time, the decision is made, and tomorrow he will enlist. Later that evening after church, Tom sits down at the piano and plays again for the trainee troops.

Monday morning Tom marches to the commanding officers hut, knocks on the door and enters.

The CO asks "yes corporal, what can I do for you?"

Tom replies after a moments silence "I'd like to enlist in the army"

"Good for you, you will need to go for a medical and all that"

"I understand. I just want to do my bit for my country".

The CO becomes a bit sterner and says "you realise that you will be a private in the regular army, and the training is much harder"

"Yes sir"

"And once you've had the medical, your entry in the army will be immediate"

"Yes sir"

"And when you enlist, it's for four years"

"Yes sir"

"Good, go to Hut D and see the doctor"

"Yes sir"

Tom salutes, turned and marches out.

He walks across the field to Hut D, walks in where he is greeted by the doctors' assistant.

"Name?" he says

"Lane" comes the reply "Thomas Lane"

"Wait here"

A few moments later he is shown into the doctor's room.

"Ah, Mister Lane. Just received a telephone call from the CO, you want to join up. Jolly good show. Stand on the white cross and read the board in front of you"

The letters are read with ease.

"Good" says the doctor "excellent eyesight. Now, take your top and boots off"

Tom sits down and takes his boots off then strips down to his bare chest as the doctor examines him, starting with his height.

"A good six feet tall; well over the limit"

The doctor carries on examining including weight, blood pressure and listening to Toms' chest with his stethoscope. He sits down and starts to write notes. As he writes he says "get dressed".

As Tom does up his tunic he is told "you're in perfect health, you couldn't be better"

"I should hope so" he says "I walk five miles a day"

"Yes" replies the doctor "a postman"

As the doctor finishes up his notes, he closes up the folder and asks Tom to wait in the waiting room. About twenty minutes later, he is called into another room.

He enters and stands to attention in front of an officer.

"Ah Lane" says the man "take this Bible"

Tom takes the book.

"Repeat after me" says the officer "I swear to serve His Majesty the King, His heirs and successors"

"I swear to serve His Majesty the King, His heirs and successors"

"And the generals and officers set over me, so help me God"

"And the generals and officers set over me, so help me God"

Tom hands back the Bible.

"Well done, you are now Private Lane, 371702"

"Thank you sir"

"Now, you will join the rest of the platoon, the Third/Eighth London Brigade. Your training starts immediately".

"YES SIR" as Tom salutes. He is now a regular soldier, "that's it" he thinks as he marches out of the hut, "I'm going to France".

Outside are the platoon, they have heard Tom was going to join up. The rest of five company are also there, having joined up previously. They clap as he comes out.

"About bloody time" shouts a soldier

His first duties are drill and marching. The platoon marches through the village, people are standing around and watching, Tom sees an old lady sitting by the road and he shouts "hello grandma". A young boy starts to march alongside Tom with a wooden stick as a pretend gun.

"Come on soldier" he says to the young lad "keep up"

The boy smiles at Tom and eventually falls back. He waves at the soldiers as they march on. The week is filled with so much, but he revels in it, there is more shooting practice and the sergeant introduces himself.

"For those of you who are new, I'm your sergeant. Sergeant Taylor."

"YES SIR" comes the reply in unison

"Now, this here is the love of your life. You keep it with you at all times. It is your Lee Enfield otherwise known as the soldiers' friend. It is more valuable to you than your mother or your wife. Hold it, keep it, cherish it but most of all, don't get it dirty.....or it won't work. In France it will be dirty' so keep it clean. CLEAN, CLEAN, CLEAN"

The soldiers continue to stand with their rifles listening to this sergeant shouting.

"So when you get to France, don't get yer rifle dirty. It won't work! What do you do?"

The soldiers reply in unison "KEEP IT CLEAN, SARGE!"

The next day isn't as much fun as it's digging duties, and the soldiers spend the day digging a trench about 20 metres long in the grass field. They fill up bags with dirt and lay them in the walls of dirt. The sergeant tells the men to get in the trench with their rifles.

"That's it lads, get a feel of your future home" he says.

Tom looks up and down the trench, then puts his foot on a sand bag in the wall and hoists himself up and looks over the top. He sees the sergeant march up to him and says "lovely view private?"

"Oh yes" says Tom smiling.

"Well, you're DEAD soldier".

He immediately comes down and loses his smile.

"What?" he says.

The sergeant explains to the whole troop "if you stick your head over the top in France you will get shot by a Boche sniper" he leans closer to Toms' face "if that German sees your lovely mug he will shoot it. Is that clear?"

"Yes Sarge" says Tom

"Remember that, it could save your life. Resist the urge to look over the top"

The next day is a bit more fun. The soldiers fill up sandbags with dirt and suspend them from trees. They line up in fives, while they rest the butt of their rifles on the ground and hold the muzzle with one hand. With the other hand, the soldiers place a bayonet on the end of their rifles and push it home. They lift up their rifles in attack pose and with the command from their sergeant they run several metres and thrust their bayonets hard into the sandbags.

"Come on" shouts the sergeant "put some effort into it, you're not inviting the enemy for tea, you want to kill him"

Tom enjoys this bit and suspects the other men do too. He imagines it is a German soldier at the receiving end of his bayonet, especially all the bad things they have done, they deserve it after all. The dirt falls out of the hole made by the bayonet but the sack doesn't empty. After a few piercings though, it does go limp, then it is replaced. This goes on for most of the day.

By the end of the week, Tom is tired. Not sleepy tired but his whole body aches. He has muscles he never knew he had that had to do work. He is glad to be home on leave, he walks from the station past the shops, looks in the window of the food market and the shop is full of people. The shelves are empty and customers are buying what's left. He carries on, desperate to get home. He hugs his wife and sits down for tea; Ellen by now knows that Tom is in the army from his letters. After tea, he does the thing he missed most, off to the pub. Although not strictly true, he did drink over the last week, but he was limited by the strict army rules. He is going to make up for it now as he walks into the pub and greets his friends, some of whom are missing. The older men are still there, Arthur, Patrick and Fred. He buys a beer, something he doesn't do very often but then most of his regular friends are away at the Front. The Kitchener poster had done its job; the men have to their bit for their country. He hands over his money and sits with some friends.

"Can you believe it?" he says "beer has gone up in price" says Tom

"Never mind" says Arthur "they'll be celebrating Christmas with us as the Germans will be defeated easily".

Patrick has a newspaper which Tom can't help notice the headline, he asks about it.

"Ah yes" says Pat "a Canadian soldier has been found crucified in a German trench"

"Yes, and they cut young women's hands off too" chips in Fred

Tom joins in "when I was at training I heard stories of how the Germans bayonet babies"

"Aw, how barbaric" says Fred

"Yes, those Germans need to be given a thrashing" says Patrick

"Oh they will" says Tom "you'll see. I've heard they're on the run".

All four men lift their glasses at nearly the same time and take a sip of their beers.

A brief silence before Arthur asks "yeah, how was your training Tom?"

"Oh great" he replies "I'm suffering for it though, I ache all over"

"Isn't it about time you joined the proper army?" demanded Fred

Tom takes another sip of his beer, looks at the other men and says "I have, look at my regimental badge", then laughs.

The others move closer to have a look, and then sit back.

"I should be going to France soon, I'm on leave"

"Good! Make sure you get a few of those Germans for us" says Pat

"Ooh I will, don't you worry"

Tom can't see behind him, but the other chaps can.

Fred points and says "Will you look at that?"

Pat turns his head slightly "Yeah, she must be on the game or something"

"What?" says Tom

"That woman, she's in here, in this pub, on her own" Says Arthur

"No? A single woman? It's not right" with that he turns round and sees Ellen wandering around looking for something. Then she stops, looks at Tom and makes her way straight to him.

"Ellen?" he enquires.

"Hello, I got bored at home. I though I'd come and join you"

"Gentlemen, this is my wife, Ellen"

The three men look uncomfortable after the things they have said, but all say hello. Then one of the men suggests Tom plays the piano, he doesn't need asking again and the group crowd around the piano while Tom plays into the night.

A few days later, he gets his suitcase and puts his uniform on; he is in the regular army now and has to leave his postal job. He is told that his job will be left open for him when he gets back. Ellen walks with him to the station and as they walked around the corner they stop on the pavement across the road from the butchers. Druhms is the name of the family business who are English with German grandparents. There is a crowd around the front of the shop, they shout and are noisy, some bricks are hurled through the window and some of the crowd climb through. The owner is pulled out and beaten up. Others are walking off with bits of meat; some furniture is thrown out of the top window with some of the families belongings. Tom and Ellen stand on the corner watching. A smile slowly comes across his face.

"That should teach those Germans, putting the price of beer up an' all"

Suddenly a piano comes flying out of the top window and crashes to the ground.

"Oh, that's a shame, that's a fine piano".

"Come on Tom, let's go" says Ellen and she pulls him along leaving the crowd to disperse as the police eventually made an appearance. They get to the station, buy a ticket and wait on the platform. As the train pull in Tom says "don't worry, I'm not going to France just yet. It's just training".

They hug then he gets in, slams the door and puts his head out of the window.

"I'll write" he says as the train starts to pull out.

CHAPTER 4

WHEN ARE WE GOING TO THE FRONT?

SERGEANT TAYLOR IS A STERN and firm fellow. He doesn't joke around he just gets on with the job. He tells the men what to do and stands for no nonsense from anyone. It doesn't mean he is aloof or arrogant, he thinks every man is important and to make a mistake at the Front can spell the end for the whole platoon. Tom stands in the line-up waiting for the sergeant to come around for inspection.

"Very nice" he says "you men have turned out to be fine soldiers. Just keep it up"

Then he moves his face close to Tom "Lane! I hear you're playing in the concert tonight"

"Yes sir"

"Well, I hope your playing is as good as your soldierin', I want to hear MUSIC"

"Oh it will be good sir"

The sergeant steps back "right, at ease!" he shouts "DISMISS!"

The soldiers walk off.

Frank walks with Tom "he's got it in for you Tom"

"Nooo, he'll just sit there entranced by the music" he turns his head to the soldier "you'll see"

"Yes well, I'm looking forward to the concert tonight too"

The concert is going well, Tom plays the piano but can't help noticing that Sergeant Taylor might not like it as the man rarely shows emotion, and the blighter is sitting on the front row! Still, the soldiers like the music, they cheer and clap and raise their glasses.

"More" they shout.

The end of the concert and the band stands up and bow. Tom steps off the low stage as the audience mingle and chat.

"Lane!" bellows Sergeant Taylor

"Sir" replies Tom

"Damn good show. You play that piano well"

"Thank you sir"

The sergeant turns to the other band members

"That was a good show men" he says.

The band is pleased.

"I'll see you tomorrow, Lane"

Sergeant Taylor walks off.

The next day, the sergeant shows them no mercy and pushes the platoon to the limit. He makes them do bayonet practice in the morning, then in the afternoon, it is physical exercise. The men are exhausted.

"Blimey!" says Frank panting as he runs "you'd have thought the concert last night would have calmed him down"

Tom turns to him "not Sergeant Taylor, he likes to see us suffer"

The sergeant bellows "no talking over there"

Tom hasn't heard from his father for a while, it is the middle of August and he has been to several places around the country for training, but Fovant is his main base. He is getting worried; the last letter said that father was going over the top. Even mother hasn't heard anything, he can do nothing but carry on with his training. For a few weeks, he has trained hard but still no word. Then one day on a fine sunny September morning, the local military postman gives Tom a letter, it looks like his mother's writing. He tears it open, reads the letter and slumps onto his bed.

"What's up Tom?" asks a fellow soldier

"It's my father" he replies

"Well?"

"He's back here in England"

"He's alive though?"

"Yes, he's in hospital, he's been gassed"

Tom manages to get leave so that he can go and visit his father in hospital. He is sent to the Beaversbrook in Brondesbury, not far from where he lives. He walks into the room and sees his father there lying still.

"Father?"

Tom senior opens his eyes and coughs.

"Son. It's nice to see you. You look good in your uniform" he coughs "it suits you well"

"What happened?"

"Damn Boche, sprayed the area full of gas"

Father coughs again

"We didn't stand a chance. The whole platoon came down"

Tom takes his father's hand for a moment

"Take it easy father"

"Well, it looks like you were right, Tom" wheezes Tom senior

"No no no, nobody could have seen this. You were right. You did your bit for the country and I'm proud of you"

Father pushes himself up a little

"Open that drawer son" he says gasping for air

Tom does, inside are his father's personal effects

"Take out the watch"

He pulls the end of the chain and eventually a pocket watch comes out dangling. He makes a motion to give the watch to his father

"No, it's yours, you have it" he wheezes.

"But father, this is the watch grandfather gave you"

Tom senior sits up a little and becomes slightly sterner "and it's now yours"

He slumps back on the pillow "just think of it as a family heirloom, alright?"

"Yes father, I'll look after it"

"Now, if I could have a little peace before your mother arrives. She can be such hard work"

"Yes father, get well soon. I have to go back to Fovant to continue my training"

The old man wheezes and lifts up a hand in farewell.

Tom gets up and walks to the door but before he opens it, he turns and says "see you later father"

He closes the door, slumps against the wall and closes his eyes. Down the corridor comes a 'clump-clump' of shoes on the hard flooring. Tom opens his eyes and looks down towards the source of the noise; it is his mother with Liz and Ada. Liz speaks first "Tom, what's up?"

"I hope I never get gassed" is all Tom can say. He walks a few steps then turns to face the three women.

"I'll be in Ellie's cafe on the Kilburn High Road, join me when you've finished. I have to go back to Fovant"

He is back at Fovant for training and the first day he is there, the troops line up for their lesson. A soldier leans his head over to Tom and whispers "how's yer father, Tom?"

Tom leans his head over and whispers back "not too bad, I think he'll make it"

The sergeant barks "men, you've got new 'ats, go and pick yours up at the stores"

The troops march off to the stores hut and each man is issued with a tin hat, then march back to the parade area.

The soldier next to Tom says "you look lovely in yours dear"

"Get out of it" he replies then jokes "do you really think so?", and then he hits the man on his helmet with his knuckles. All laugh as the rest of the men put on their new helmets. The sergeant comes along and shouts "the army has issued you with new 'ats. When you get to the Front you will wear them at all times, they will save your lives".

What the soldiers haven't noticed is a pile of equipment nearby on the grass.

"Now you ladies 'ave finished admiring yourselves, we 'ave gas training"

The sergeant picks up one of the pieces of equipment. It is a box into which he puts his hand; he pulls out a face mask with two glass eye holes. Joining the two is a hose.

"This gentlemen is your new gas mask, a box respirator. Better than the old one and more durable. The hun are using a new kind of gas that is more lethal than the previous one..."

The sergeant's face becomes more serious than normal,

"So we are going to spend the day doing gas drill. Now pick yourself a mask"

Tom fears the gas even though he has never experienced it, seeing his father is enough to put him off. The soldiers go over to the pile and pick up a box each then gradually move back into formation. The sergeant straps his box to his chest, the soldiers follow suit. Another soldier is standing nearby next to a bell mounted on a branch of a tree.

"When you hear the alarm" says the sergeant as he turns to the soldier, who then starts to ring the bell briefly,

"You pull out your mask" which he does, "and slide the mask over your head"

He pulls the mask easily over his head, and with a heavily muffled voice he tells the troops to put their masks on. The sergeant takes his mask off and asks the soldiers to also take theirs off. He pulls out a stopwatch and says "now, I'm going to time you. I want you to get your masks on in seven seconds. Do you hear me?"

"YES SERGEANT"

"Seven seconds now" a pause as he holds up his watch "GAS! GAS! GAS!"

The men fumble with their masks, some dropping the mask on the floor but eventually getting on their protective

47

headgear. As the last man finishes the sergeant stops his watch.

"That was pathetic. Take your masks off and we'll try that again"

Bong, bong, bong goes the bell and the men go through the procedure again. And again. And again. They keep doing it until the sergeant is happy that the men can perform the operation flawlessly in the time required.

"That's it. You lovely ladies are getting BETTER!"

The soldiers are relieved; they drop their masks on the floor.

"Who said we've finished?" bellows the sergeant

"We'll keep going until you can do it in your sleep"

The platoon carry on with gas training for the rest of the afternoon.

With training ended for the day, Tom sits down under the trees with a view of the hill. He knows that tomorrow will be gas training again, and probably the next day too. He looks at the badges in the side of the hill and pulls out pen and paper from his bag then starts to write:

"Dearest Ellen"

He stops and puts his pen to his mouth.

"I hope this letter finds you well. We have been busy training today and I'm tired. We have been putting gas masks on and off all day. You know, the lads call the mask a goggle-eyed booger. Funny name, even so, I hate them. I can't get the image of my father out of my head.

I have made some new friends here. There's Frank Herbert from near us, somewhere in Willesden. I don't know him but he knows me. Then there's Joseph Newell, he's from Kent. Frank and Joe get on like a house on fire; they are always ribbing each other.

There is still no news about whether we go to the Front yet but I don't mind telling you, I am a little scared. Still, for King and country, I will do my duty.

Your loving husband, Tom"

Wednesday December the 13th, Liz is getting married to Bertie. Tom is there on leave, not in uniform though but he does wear his regimental badge on his breast pocket. Back at home where the reception takes place, Tom shakes Bertie by the hand,

"Congratulations Bertie" he says

"Thanks Tom"

"I hope she's as kind to you as she was to me"

"What do you mean?" asks Liz

"Sis, you know I'm only joking. I hope you two will be happy together and well done"

He kisses his sister on the cheek

"Now!" he says "where's the drink?"

He marches over to the beer barrel and pours himself a drink. His mother eyes him suspiciously. Tom turns and says "hello mother"

He walks over to his father who is now out of hospital, but still looks ill

"How are you father?"

"Better, much better"

"Are you out of the army now?"

"Yes, they found out my age. A bit late really"

"Yes" says Tom "they should have stopped you joining in the first place"

"Oh, you don't mean that"

"We-ell, I'm just glad you're back"

"You're not off to the Front yet then?"

"No word"

The two men sup their beer

Tom doesn't go back to Fovant and stays on leave for Christmas, after nearly a year of training, he is enjoying this time off. He decides he'll pop into the sorting office to see his old colleagues.

"Hello Tom" says Vernon "you on leave?"

"Yes, for Christmas"

"So, you're not at the Front yet?" asks Ralph

"No, I'm still waiting for my orders. I've heard the German army is about to collapse, I'll probably help mop up the mess afterwards"

"Eh, you'll kill a few Germans for us, won't you?" cuts in Lionel

The postal workers put on their coats.

"Fancy a pint Tom? We're going down to the pub" says Ralph

"No, not me. Not yet, I'm going home first, my wife's cooking dinner.....and then down the pub"

The little party get to the first pub and it's full of merry revellers right up to the front door.

"Oh, it's full, next pub lads" shouts Vernon

They cross over the Kilburn High Road and head down Kilburn Park Road discussing the new Prime minister and their plans for Christmas. Just past the underground station to the next pub, the Prince of Wales, which is also full.

"Oh bad luck" says Tom

"Never mind, onward to the Carlton" says Vernon

Tom says "this is where I turn off. You chaps have a good time and have a good Christmas"

"Don't you worry' we will. You have a good one too Tom" says Lionel

Tom turns right down Carlton Vale while the small party turn left going down the opposite way. He turns round and sees the men walk through the door of the pub and he smiles to himself.

"I can see those boys getting themselves into trouble with their wives"

In the distance Tom can hear a droning. He's heard a similar noise before with aeroplanes, but this sounds different. He turns round and sees either a plane in the distance or an extremely large plane that was closer. It has distinctive black crosses on the wings and there are explosions following it.

"German bomber planes"

He rushes to the nearest cover he can find. It is a Gotha plane, Germany's newest weapon. He looks in horror as the bombs explode down Carlton Vale, and then blow up the pub then the plane continues north-west destroying houses in its path as it flies on.

"NO" shouts Tom. He runs towards the pile of rubble that was once 'The Carlton'. He scrabbles at bricks and throws them behind him. People are now coming out of their houses and joining in with the rescue effort.

Fire engines are now appearing and Tom's hands are getting cut from the rubble but he won't give up, the firemen join in with the rescue. After two hours, several bodies have been recovered and laid on the ground, covered up and lifeless. Tom stands there with his hands in his pockets brooding. To think, only a few hours ago he was having a conversation with them.

He walks home wearily and relays the events to Ellen. He has trouble eating his food but after a while he manages it.

"And just before Christmas as well" he says "I'm going to give those Germans what for when I see them"

Ellen has a worried look on her face. All she can think about is Tom being shot at by the enemy and being brought back in a body bag.

CHAPTER 5

AT LAST. WE'RE ON OUR WAY

IT IS NOW A FEW months into 1917, the war hasn't finished. If anything, the war is continuing stronger than ever. The Germans have dug themselves in around Ypres in Flanders. The French have mutinied; the British have made minor gains, as for Tom he's still in England, still training and has been for the whole of 1916. Everyday life in Britain carried on; people were reluctant to let the Germans win. "Business as usual" became a common phrase used in civilian life.

He has formed an army band with other recruits and plays to packed houses both military and public alike. But now is the time in April as he has received his orders to go, the platoon lines up as sergeant Taylor walks up and down the line.

"You lucky, lucky people are going to the Front" he barks.

"Now go and enjoy your leave and be back at your meeting point for eight o'clock sharp on Wednesday."

With that, troops walk in different directions as each have their own destinations.

Tom is spending his final leave with his wife; he turns up at the house and knocks on the door as he wants to surprise Ellen. She answers it with joy on her face even though she knew her husband would be home soon. They walk in together and sit down.

"Ooh it's lovely to see you back".

He replies "that it is" then pauses while looking down.

"What is it Tom?" she asks.

"I have to go Southampton the day after tomorrow to prepare for our trip to the Front, I thought it would be good idea to go down to the Falcon and see some friends"

A quick cup of tea and they walk down Malvern Road to the pub. Inside Tom heads straight for the bar but is accosted before he gets there.

"Hello Tom, where've you been lately?"

"I've been training"

"And when do you go?"

"The day after tomorrow, I sail from Southampton in a few days time"

Another man shouts "Tom" as he grabs him by the arm and yanks him forcibly towards the piano.

"Give us a tune then"

"Yeah, come on, you know our favourites"

And the crowd gets excited.

"Alright" says Tom surveying all the faces as they start to calm down. He sweeps his hand across the top of the piano and says "line them up", he sits down and within seconds pints of beer appear on the top of the piano as people return from the bar. People start singing as Ellen sits down on the stool next to Tom; he plays with one hand and drinks with the other. The joyous singing goes on until the pub closes.

The next day is spent seeing family and Tom is especially happy to see his father. His mother still looks as sour as ever but Liz and her husband Thomas are there, as is Ada and her husband Charlie. Uncle Albert as well. Although Grandfather isn't there, he finds it difficult to get out and about nowadays and can't handle social affairs. Everyone comments on how handsome Tom looks in his uniform and asks when he was going to the Front.

"Our brother is a soldier" says Liz

"Yes, he'll see the Germans off" says Ada

Tom senior walks up and takes his son by the shoulders

"Tom, I know what it's like out there. You look after yourself. Try not to get yourself gassed, it's not nice"

Uncle Albert comes along and guides people to line up for a photograph.

Everyone poses. "Poof" goes the flash; everyone relaxes and heads for their drinks. Uncle Albert speaks to Tom "go and see your Grandfather, I'm sure he'd like to see you before you go away"

Tom tells Ellen where he is going and says he won't be long, he walks to Grandfather's house and is shown in by Mr Greene, the landlord.

"Hello Grandfather" he says

"TOM!" says Grandfather William "how nice to see you"

"How are you Grandfather?" asks Tom

"Oh you know, I'm fine. My body's a little creaky but I'm doing alright. Don't you look something in your uniform? Come on; let's have a look at you"

The old man adjusts his spectacles and examines his grandson.

"You're a soldier now, when do you go?"

"Tomorrow, I go to Southampton tomorrow. The boat leaves the day after that"

"Hmm. I hope you look after yourself, it's not nice over there you know"

"I know but we have to see off the Germans"

"Well, whatever happens, you'll come back as a hero, just like your father"

"I hope so"

Grandfather points to a bottle of wine on the table

"Open up that bottle and we'll have a celebratory drink, eh?"

Tom opens it up and pours two glasses "just a quick one, I said I would be back at the party"

"Here's to our Country's victory" says Grandfather and both men raise their glasses.

The following morning Tom gets up, has a wash, and shaves in the kitchen then goes to the bedroom and puts his uniform on. He stands to look at himself in the mirror. He then picks up the pocket watch and attaches the chain then slips the watch into his breast pocket. He turns to and sees a photograph. He stops for a moment, and then he picks up the photograph. It is a picture of Ellen. He smiles at the image of his wife then puts the photograph in his breast pocket. He pats the pocket with his right hand, then stands to attention and salutes to himself in the mirror.

"For King and Country" he says then walks out of the bedroom.

Ellen has also got up while he was getting ready, washes and is preparing breakfast. At the breakfast table Ellen asks Tom where he has to go.

"We go to Southampton for a few days for a brief training, and then it's on the boat to France"

Ellen looks down and pushes her food around with her fork.

"Don't worry Ellen. I'll be alright" he says "I won't be over there long; I've heard we've got the Germans on the run".

It doesn't help. Although Ellen is proud her husband is doing his bit for the country, she feels apprehensive about him going, after all, she knows many women who have lost their husbands and sons at the Front. The pair finish breakfast and while Ellen washes up, Tom gets his kit ready. They both make their way to the train station; take the train from Queens Park to Baker Street, then to Waterloo. The train is ready, troops are milling around with their wives and mothers. Tom throws his kit into the carriage then turns to look at Ellen. The two look at each other then embrace. It is a sight that isn't out of place as the same scene is going on up and down the platform.

The whistle blows and all the couples withdraw from each other and the soldiers step onto the train. The doors slam shut and a row of heads stick out the windows. The huge engine starts to slowly pull its cargo out of the station. The women along the platform stand and wave to their respective partner or son. The soldiers all wave back as the train slowly pulls away, Ellen drops her hand as a tear rolls down her cheek.

Tom has been in Southampton for two days waiting around, although it isn't really waiting, lots of drill and marching. But now the time has come as he stands on the deck of the ship. The 'SS Huntscraft' slowly pulls out of harbour; he looks down at the port as the crowd cheers and waves. Southampton slowly shrinks out of sight as he realises this is it, this is the real thing, the war. He recalls all the stories he's heard of soldiers going to the Front and whole regiments being wiped out. "Will I see Ellen again" he thinks to himself.

He turns to look at the deck of the ship. Soldiers are milling around everywhere, playing cards, sleeping or just chatting. He sees Frank and Joe sitting together playing cards, arguing as usual but Tom is glad they came along. He then turns and looks out to sea in the direction of France, he is still standing in the same place an hour later when another soldier stands next to him, also deep in thought. Finally the soldier says "well, this is it, we're on our way".

"Yes, but will we get there?" says Tom

"What do you mean?" asks the soldier

"Well, the German submarines are patrolling these waters. I mean, look what happened to the Lusitania"

"Yeah, sunk with all hands on board"

"That was torpedoed by a German submarine you know"

The soldier thinks for a bit "at least it got the Americans into the war now"

The two soldiers introduce themselves.

"Where are you going?" asks Tom

"France" replies the soldier

"What a coincidence, so am I"

The two men laugh.

"My name's Charles Fletcher" he says as he offers an out-stretched hand "call me Charlie"

The two shake "I'm Thomas Lane, just Tom will do"

After a few hours, the ship makes it to France and slowly glides into Le Havre. The troops disembark and make their way to the signing in stations. Now begins the journey to Paris. "Paris" he thinks out loud, "I never been to Paris" he says as he turns to the soldier next to him. The platform is packed with soldiers, Tom notices a hand painted sign pinned to the wall that reads "this way to the trenches" with an arrow underneath.

The soldiers stay in Paris for a few days sitting around outside cafes, drinking and chatting. Tom, Frank, Joe and Charlie introduce themselves to two soldiers who have been with them since the boat.

"I'm Archie Haywood"

"And I'm Edward Spencer from Battle"

Archie continues "we met in the Post Office Rifles"

Tom tells them that he too is from the same organisation. A woman walks past the small troop.

"Oh, the French women" remarks Charlie

"Easy now" says Tom "you're married"

"Aw, she won't know"

The men sit around laugh and sup their drinks.

"There's the Eiffel Tower" says Ed

Tom looks up "I think we should go up there"

"What for?" says Archie

"We're here in Paris. You cannot go to Paris and not go up the Eiffel Tower"

"Is it open?"

Tom stands up "let's go and find out, eh?"

The troops get the train to Rouen.

"Well then" says Tom "wasn't the view worth it"

"It was alright I s'pose" replies Charlie

"What's the matter with you man? The view was fantastic"

Archie pipes up "yuh, but all those stairs? I'm worn out now"

"I don't care" says Tom "it was worth going up the tower"

At Rouen, the soldiers get off the train and begin their long march up to Arras.

"Me legs are killing me" says Archie

"Quit complaining" Tom scolds the soldier "we're on our way now, to the trenches. This is it lads, the war"

Once the soldiers reach their destination they begin their trench training immediately. Digging holes, rifle training and most importantly, gas mask training. That all important seven seconds.

Thursday June the seventh, orders are to get up at two-thirty in the morning. The soldiers are to wait with their guns at the ready. Tom looks across the clearing at Ed, Archie and Charlie who are all poised for anything. He can't see Frank and Joe but he knows they are nearby somewhere.

"What time is it?" asks a young soldier who looks too young to be here.

Tom pulls his watch out of his pocket "a minute to three"

"Oh" says the young man. Young inexperienced soldiers often attach themselves to older more experienced soldiers who are known as 'Old Sweats', although Tom isn't so he gives the impression he is to the lad.

"Me name's Cecil" says the young man "Cecil Barton from Wisbech"

"Tom" comes the reply "Tom Lane...from Kilburn"

Cecil continues the conversation "I was a postman, thought I'd join up, see some action"

"Humm!" replies Tom as if put out by the young lad's reason for joining up.

"You know" continues Cecil "I want to kill some Germans, especially after what they've done to our country"

Tom can see soldiers are standing around behind whatever solid object they can find. No one knows what to expect, an attack perhaps.

"Tom, what..."

"Five past three" cuts in Tom without looking at his watch.

At ten minutes past three, just as Cecil is about to ask the time again an enormous explosion is heard the ground shakes. At the same time the soldiers witness a huge flame extending into the air, over 200 metres high. At the base of the flame is a bright white light. In less than a minute, the Germans respond with a barrage of shell fire.

As the explosion dies down, a Commanding Officer shouts "get ready, prisoners will be coming in soon".

As the sun starts to rise, the barrage continues off in the distance and although a few miles off, the noise is horrendous. Within the hour, the commotion dies down and lines of German soldiers arrive with their hands on their heads. Many look dishevelled, some are bleeding. Tom and his friend stand there ready with their guns. This is the first time either of them have seen German soldiers and the hatred wells up inside them.

"There they are Tom, the devils themselves" says Cecil

But Tom just carries on looking while the enemy soldiers are led away to the internment camp and the order comes to stand down.

June the thirtieth. News has reached the platoon what had happened that day. Apparently, an engineer force had dug tunnels underneath the German trenches and laid thousands of pounds of explosives in the tunnels. The explosion tore through the German defences sending bodies flying for hundreds of metres. Those that had survived, the men Tom had seen being marched in, were so demoralised that they just gave themselves up. Now the British are winning and Tom feels happy, he may be going home soon. He is busy moving jerry cans full of water when a formation of four planes flies overhead high in the sky.

The planes are Gotha bombers. The Germans are using a new tactic instead of the zeppelins, which are slow and inaccurate. These planes are bigger and heavier, and can carry a larger load. They are also faster and can therefore fly during the day. Tom has seen a Gotha in action before last Christmas; his heart sinks because he knows where they are going and what they can do. The planes fly over the white cliffs, over Kent and head for London. The formation splits into two, one set of two flies to South London while the other heads north.

Ellen decides this day she will go shopping in Paddington, there are some grocery stores she knows of that will have some food on their shelves for certain. She first hears the Gothas and stands wondering what they are. Luckily she is way down the street when the bomb hits the grocery store. Glass and rubble flies quite a distance across the street. From the dust staggers a woman who is coughing and spluttering. Ellen rushes to her aid as other people gather around.

She gasps "my husband and children are in there".

Ellen tries to comfort the woman as a man comes out with a dead child in his arms, quickly followed by another man, also with a dead boy. The woman cries in anguish, a man standing close by says "damn Germans, they should all be killed"

Another man replies "that's alright, our boys will see to them in Belgium".

Of course, none of this helps the woman who Ellen tries desperately to comfort.

Back in Arras, Tom and his platoon are moving supplies again when a platoon of soldiers march wearily into town. They are the remains of the 8th London Regiment who Tom will be joining on the Front. The army consists of a few hundred soldiers marching past, the new soldiers knowing that this regiment should be a few thousand strong. It started of as two regiments and this is all that is left, the first and second regiments joined together to form just the 8th. Tom recognises one of the soldiers from five company of the Post Office Rifles, it was William Harvey. They greet each other.

"How are you" says Tom

"Tired, you'll see, when you get there, you'll see" says Bill

Tom replies "never mind that, we've managed to get a band together. We're playing tonight. Are the others with you?"

Bill hangs his head "dead. All dead"

"Yeah, all of them. Dead" complains a soldier behind Bill

"This is Andy Beal" says Bill

"Pleased to meet you" says Andy sounding like he didn't mean what he said.

"Pleasure" says Tom

Bill continues "and this chap is Harry Mansfield"

"How do?" says Harry shaking Tom's hand

The evening comes and Tom is with the quickly assembled band and they play to the war weary troops, who after months of fighting appreciate the concert.

CHAPTER 6

THE TRENCHES AT WIPERS

THE NEXT DAY, THE PLATOON is ready to move out; Tom picks up his kit and joins the troop along with the other new soldiers, the young lad stays close to Tom.

Bill says "here we go, we're off to Wipers"

"Wipers?" asks Tom

"He means Ypres" Says Andy

"Yeah, Wipers. Blown to bits, nothing left of it" replies Bill

Andy starts to complain "I don't want to go to Ypres"

He starts to behave irrationally "I've got a wife and kids, I don't want to go"

Bill says "easy man, we don't want to go either. But we have to"

"Yeah well, I can sympathise with him" complains Charlie

And they go; Andy calms down and they finally get to Ypres or what is left of it. There are remnants of buildings here and there that say it is a town but the actual landmarks and buildings are gone, not much to guide anyone around. What was the Cloth Hall is now rubble and only people who knew the town intimately could maybe point out what each building used to be. To the soldiers it is a ghost town, eerie and silent. It has been raining for the last two days and everywhere is muddy and finally after an hour walk the countryside appears, although it can't really be called it that. The trees are just stumps with the land totally devoid of plants, it is just mud.

The platoon stops at an old farmhouse known to the Tommies as Springfield Farm. There are several large tents around which are the sleeping quarters for the troops, the farmhouse is the HQ although it is quite battered and there is a train line close by with some empty carriages on the tracks. The front line trench is less than two hundred metres away; Tom says to himself "that's where I'll be going tomorrow".

Cecil overhears and replies "yes, and we can have a pop at Boche, eh?"

Charlie leans over "don't get so keen, lad"

The landscape in the distance is of desolation, there are few landmarks as everything has been bombed out of existence while over the horizon are hordes of balloons floating in the sky. Four officers walk in to the tent, the commanding Officer talks first.

"Welcome to Ypres gentlemen"

The troops are introduced to their new commanding officers,

"This is your sergeant, Sergeant Knight"

"Evening men" the sergeant says with a Brummie accent.

"Lance Corporal Bennett"

"Evening"

"And Lance Corporal Addiscott"

"Evening"

After the evening meal (bully beef) Tom settles down to sleep, the bombs going off constantly at the Front, which, he thinks to himself, is not very far away. This worry keeps him thinking about the possibility of being hurt, and keeps him awake. Cecil is in a bed next to Tom and can't stop fidgeting, further disturbing his colleague's sleep. Finally, the bombs stop and Tom falls asleep. However, the thought keeps nagging away at his mind, and he drifts in and out of sleep. In the early hours of the morning, the bombing starts again.

Thursday August the second and Tom gets up feeling awful, he had hardly any sleep during the night and decides after breakfast he will try and write a letter. He learns very quickly that the bombing carries out mainly at dusk and dawn although this isn't a set rule and can happen at any time without warning. However, before he can get pen to paper he sees that a train in the distance is coming up the track and stops. Tom gets up and walks closer. The train driver is standing on the footplate talking to an officer.

The officer asks "why have you stopped here? The depot is at the end there"

"Monsieur, I go no further. Au revoir"

And with that the driver reverses back down the track. The officer calls men over, including Tom and organises them so some are pushing the first carriage and some pull. They slowly inch their way up the two hundred metres of track to the waiting depot, and then once secured, they start to unload the rations inside. Behind them, another platoon of men does the same with the next carriage, then another platoon for the third carriage. The shelling starts again, Tom thinks the train driver wise to get going. The men load the crates on the floor while others open the crates, inside are shells, they then start to fill up bags that are strapped to mules. Tom has the task of leading a mule to pull a wagon to the front guns, Cecil joins in with help. The animal strains with the heavy load and starts to move, with Tom at the reins and the young lad pushing the cart. He gingerly manoeuvres the wagon along the duck-board with the wheels just inside the edges. He guides the mule and moves from side to side to check the wheels are within the edges of the board.

A shell explodes twenty metres away sending mud everywhere and, lucky for the men, the shrapnel misses them. Tom is covered by the wagon but he takes a look at the side, embedded into the wood are pieces of hot metal. He quickly moves round and grabs the reins and notices the boy cowering behind the wagon with his arms covering his face.

"Cecil! Get up!"

The lad stands up and puts his hands on the back of the cart.

"Come on mate, move yourself" Tom says to the animal.

Another bomb goes off again but closer and the noise scares the mule. It pulls and jerks, and then it screeches while Tom tries to calm it down. It is too late as one of the wheels touches the edge and goes over, which is enough to drag the whole wagon and mule over into the mud. Cecil stands back not knowing what to do. The mule kicks and squirms, and the more it does, the more it sinks into the mud. Tom pulls at the reins while an officer comes over.

"Come on boy, help me!"

"There's no point, let it go" says the officer as he pulls out his revolver from its holster, points at the frightened mule and fires a bullet directly through its head. Tom and Cecil stands bewildered while the officer says "right, get this duck-board repaired and get the next wagon, we need to get these shells to the guns".

Tom starts to walk when Cecil says "where are you going?"

"Get another mule and wagon"

"But…but…he just shot the poor animal"

Tom stops, hangs his head and says "I know" then walks off leaving Cecil standing with a bewildered look.

The next day is the same, noisy evening and morning, and mud everywhere. Tom is tired but sleeps a bit better than the previous evening. He is doing mundane but necessary duties again of moving ammunition and food, when he hears a droning noise. Bombs go off a way off but close enough for worry. A German fighter plane is spotted and the soldiers immediately rush into action. Lewis guns are pulled out and placed in shell holes. They fire at the plane as it flies overhead, the anti-aircraft guns also firing. Tom and his fellow soldiers run to the nearest shell holes, trying to avoid the bullets from the planes' machine guns. The plane suffers a hit, causing smoke to pour out of the engine. It splutters before flying low and drops to the point of crashing. The flimsy contraption crashes into the ground with a thud as the tail of the plane shoots up. The pilot sits dazed for a moment before regaining enough senses to start climbing out. Masses of British soldiers run to the plane and grab the German pilot, pulling him out of his cockpit.

Cecil turns his head to Tom while saying "come on Tom, it's a Boche. We can punish him"

The lad runs while Tom stands looking, not knowing whether to join the throng or not. The soldiers start to pound the pilot with their fists just as officers run up behind the mob. The first officer pulls out his revolver and fires it into the air, the crowd stop immediately.

"Step away from that man" he yells

"But he's a German" comes the reply from a soldier

"Yes, he deserves to be punished" says Cecil

"He is now a prisoner of war" says the officer, and with the help of the other officers, leads the German away to a tent. The soldiers look glum but carry on grudgingly with their duties.

The next day, Tom and a small group of fellow soldiers are ordered to do trench duties. After getting their gear ready the platoon of twelve soldiers make their way to the communication trench, then through the reserve trench, and finally the front trench. Their Sergeant, Alfred Knight barks his orders. Tom thinks to himself that the enemy trench is only about a hundred metres away. Trench duties are mundane; he spends the night walking up and down the trench on sentry, in the rain trying his hardest to stay awake, his overcoat starts to soak through. Every now and then a flare goes up from the enemy, the soldiers have to lie flat against the sides of the corrugated iron wall of the trench to avoid being seen and stay there until the flare dies down, then they carry on. As Tom walks along the trench he meets another soldier also on sentry duty, a large man named Robert McKenzie from Newcastle. He had been a miner since fourteen before joining the Post Office to become a postman. Being a miner gave him his huge bulk of a body, people call him Big Bob. As Tom begins to turn he says to the other soldier "this infernal rain, when will it stop?"

The big man just shrugs his shoulders and turns back down the trench, he was never a man of words.

Tom, with his rifle that had his bayonet fixed to, stands and looks up and down the trench. The corrugated iron that holds up the soil. The wall that is on the side of the Front is taller than the other wall. He tries not to think about it but every now and then, flashes enter his mind that he will have to go over that wall. Hanging up the other side is the gas bell; it is an empty shell with the flat end removed and inside hangs a chain with a ball. Tom thinks about the re-use of materials, but the bell hangs there ominously, he hopes it will never have to ring as it reminds him of when his father was gassed. At eleven o'clock Sergeant Knight comes along and tells Tom he is relieved of sentry duty and is replaced by another.

"Have fun" says Tom

"I'm enjoying it already" replies Charlie sarcastically

Sergeant Knights sends Harry to replace Bob.

Tom makes his way back to the reserve trench into a small dugout to settle down for something to eat. He pulls back the curtain that is hanging across the doorway and walks in, quickly followed by Big Bob.

"Ah, you've just reminded me lads" says one of the soldiers sitting inside.

Tom props his rifle up against the wall, put away his bayonet and takes off his wet coat to hang up, as does Bob. Bill picks up a container with a push handle on the top; it is a converted crop sprayer. With the other hand, Bill points a hose towards the curtain and sprays it. It is vermorel spray to neutralise gas. The curtain is there for protection in the event of a gas attack when soldiers are asleep, to give them a little bit of extra time to get their masks on. The soldier put the container back and sits down to finish off his tea.

A parcel waits for Tom; he tears open the lid and pulls out a letter, as he slips onto his bunk he starts to read the letter. There is no real news, just everything is alright but times are hard, food is getting scarce, stuff that Tom knows about already. That isn't the point; the letter from Ellen means so much to Tom, it is his connection to home, as it is for so many soldiers who receive letters from loved ones. As he reads his letter, he starts to eat his meal which consists of a tin of bully beef, some cheese and jam, hard biscuits to go with sweetened tea, which is the same meal for all the lads who sit around in the dugout.

"Huh, jam again" is the complaint from Bob "we've had jam ever since we've been here"

Tom still has his partially-opened parcel next to him, his colleagues urge him to see what is in it.

"It might be something nice" says Bill

He picks up the parcel and put his hand in.

"It's from my Ellen" he says as his hand feels something familiar.

He stops and looks in, he starts to laugh.

"What" says Bill "what is it?"

"Yes Tom, what has she sent you?"

He pulls out the item and says "a jar of jam"

The rest of the gang start to laugh. Much needed relief from the turmoil of war.

The soldiers start to talk about what they will do when the war is over. Most are going to return to the work they left behind, most are sure that their jobs will be left open for them. Frank and Joe are playing cards in the far corner, arguing as they normally do.

Bill starts by saying "I just want to get out of this stinking war"

Andy nods and replies an agreement

"I've only been here since the beginning of the year, and I'm sick of it"

Andy says "yeah, sick of it"

"Still, if I'm lucky enough to get through then I'll go back to posting letters"

Ed says he just wants to get back to Battle

"What, you already fought?" says Charlie

"No! Battle, it's a village in Sussex. That's where I'm from"

Charlie screws his face up "strange name for a village"

"Hey" replies Ed "it's probably the most famous village in the country"

Charlie sits up "famous for what?"

"It's where the Battle of Hastings took place"

"But that was at Hastings"

"No, the battle took place just north of Hastings. There wasn't a village there at the time; that came later"

Charlie replies with an "ooh" like he's not really interested in history.

Bob says "I just can't wait to go home, away from this hell-hole"

The other soldiers nod in agreement.

"What about you Cecil?"

"I'll probably go back to being a postman"

"You sound like you don't like it"

"It's alright, but I wanted to come here to fight the enemy. I'll be hero when I go back"

"Is that all you want?"

"Yes. My parents are farmers, I'm a postman. I want more. You know, excitement and all that sort of stuff"

"Well if its excitement you want, you're in the right place"

"Too right. I'll get me some Germans" says Cecil

"What about you Tom?"

"Oh I think I will play in a big band and become a star"

The soldiers laugh.

"Yes, I seen you play. You're good" says a soldier bringing the laughter to a halt

"How long have you played the piano then Tom?"

"Oh since I was a boy. I was made to have lessons. I'm glad I did now because I love playing. You know, at one time, we were moving house. They lifted the piano on the back of this cart, and piled the rest of our belongings on there as well. As the horse was about to pull away, I was lifted onto the back of the cart and made to play the piano. What a sight, this horse'n'cart travelling down the road with me playing the old Joanna, people came out of their houses to watch me go past"

"Weren't you a postman?"

"Yes, and I enjoy the job. I'm hoping that soon I'll have enough money to buy a car"

"A car?"

"Yes, I love mechanical things. I would love to drive through town in my car"

"What kind of car would you like?"

"A big black shiny one"

The soldiers laugh.

Tom settles back in his bunk. He nibbles a piece of cheese but is so tired he starts to drift off.

"I wouldn't fall asleep with your food out like that, Tom" says Bill

"Mmmm" was all Tom can say as he falls into a deep sleep.

He dreams of happier times of when he was a postman. He likes that job, especially when he used to make friends with the dogs. He also thinks of Ellen. He imagines the dogs again, turns to Ellen and laughs. But the dog eats the chocolate in Toms' hand and keeps licking. He brushes off the dog and tells it that is enough but the dog keeps licking and licking, but Tom keeps brushing the dog off. He is starting to wake up now, but still feels the touch of the dogs' tongue on his hand.

"Get off" he says in a mock telling off, "you've had enough chocolate".

He is coming round now and brushes his chest, but the feeling is still there. There are no dogs here, what is it? He looks down and there on his chest eating his cheese is a pack of rats. He jumps up while letting out a cry while the cheese drops to the floor but the rats won't go away, they carry on eating the cheese. The other men laugh especially

Bob who hasn't shown much joy since coming here. Tom he looks at them in mock anger, and then he lies back on the bunk, brushes off the remaining food on his chest and falls into a deep sleep.

Tom has a good sleep until the barrage starts again in the early hours of the morning. He is on duty again at dawn so there is no point in trying to sleep more. He gets up and goes through his kit. During these bouts of shelling soldiers get scared. No one can hear each other talk and some men silently pray. On hearing the initial whistle of the shell coming over it seems like hours. When the shell explodes it is a further two seconds before the shrapnel comes over. The noise of the hot pieces of metal make a 'ring ting' noise on the tin roof of the dugout. After going through his kit for the umpteenth time the shelling stops, then all the men laugh together. Tom picks up his rifle and put his tin hat on and steps outside. The sun is coming up but the sky is still grey from the powder off the explosions.

The order comes for inspection. The men line up while the sergeant stands to attention while the Commanding Officers walk in, Lance-Corporals Addiscott and Bennett. The three men look up and down the men, check their equipment is war worthy. They randomly pick up one of the soldiers rifle and checks the bolt moves back and forth smoothly then he checks the gas masks by asking the soldiers to remove them from their chest bags for closer inspection. Once satisfied the troops are dismissed and the two Lance-corporals go on their way back to HQ, this happens every morning and evening. Now it is Tom's turn for sentry duty again, he walks up and down the trench while other soldiers are milling around doing similar tasks, carrying ammunition back and forth.

"How long was it that I had a decent bath?" he thinks to himself.

He is itching so bad and stands with his back against the trench wall and rubs his back up and down, he can't take his jacket off as it is forbidden to take items of clothing off at the front.

"Aw, me back" he says to Bob.

"Yeah, that'll be the lice" replies the big man

Tom tries to carry on as usual, the dirt and the mud, if it wasn't for this duckboard he would be walking in water. The pumps do their job but only up to a point. Although it is August, it has rained almost continuously although today the rain has stopped but it is still damp. Tom has a brief shiver then carries on walking. Frank and Joe are standing in a corner section of the trench.

"Morning chaps" says Tom to the soldiers, trying to be cheery "lovely day"

"Yeah, an' me Mam's making me a lovely roast dinner" says Frank

Tom understands the sarcasm, this is a hell hole, and if it isn't the damp then the boredom kills. The officers try to get the men to do anything, even if it is mundane work, just to keep the soldiers occupied. Tom comes across the young lad who is climbing up the wall.

"You shouldn't be doing that Cecil" he scolds the boy.

"I just want to have a look" he replies.

Just then, Sergeant Knight comes along.

"Soldier, get down from there!" he bellows.

The boy turns his head down to look at the sergeant just as he hears his helmet ring which causes him to fall to the duck-board. The two men help him up as the sergeant picks up the helmet; a piece at the side is missing with cracks radiating out from the broken section.

"You had a near miss then" says the sergeant.

The boy looks confused.

Sergeant Knight explains "that section that's missing is due to an enemy sniper bullet"; he moves closer to the boy "you could have been shot"

He straightens up and says a bit louder "don't....look.... over....the....top. Understand?"

The boy nods. He gives a quick glance to Tom then says to the boy "now go to reserves and get yourself a new helmet!"

The boy runs off down the trench with his broken helmet in his hand.

"Anything to report Private?" enquires the sergeant but before Tom can answer, shells start to rain down.

The soldiers in the trench brace themselves for the explosions, mud flies everywhere and rattle on the soldiers helmets, after a few minutes the shelling peters out. The soldiers slowly stand up with relief of no more exploding shells. Sergeant Knight walks up and down the trench as he usually does everyday. Frank and Joe are still in the corner section when a shell lands right by their feet and they recoil in horror as the shell makes a plop sound. There is no explosion, the Frank says laughingly "hey don't worry, this one's a dud".

Sergeant Knight however recognises the shell and bellows "GAS! GET YOUR MASKS ON!"

Soldiers in ear shot needn't be told a second time and immediately get their gas masks out of their bags and put them in the same fashion they had done in training hundreds of times. Bill has heard the command and starts frantically ringing the bell. However, it is too late for the Frank and Joe as they are right next to the shell and within seconds start to gasp for air. They fumble for their masks but they can't get them out in time, and fall to their knees choking. They are taken away for medical treatment but being so close, they got almost maximum dosage; they will be dead in a few days.

The rest of the soldiers in the trench have to carry on, there is no going away. The temptation to take off the masks is great, they are uncomfortable and breathing is difficult. Tom stands there with his gun along with other soldiers, at the ready although not knowing what for. The alarm call is sent to the rear and within twenty minutes, men turn up with their containers and spray all along the trench with vermorel spray, the troops are ordered to stay out of the dugouts. It seems liked forever but after a few hours the all clear is given, the soldiers can take their gas masks off. There are sighs of relief all round as the men can breathe properly again, with sweat dripping down their faces. The masks can be so claustrophobic.

The troops are told not to touch the walls of the trench as the gas is still there.

"If it's still there Sarge, then why have we taken our masks off?" asks Tom

"Because the gas has been blown away but the residue has soaked into the soil. If it stays there then it'll stay there"

Unfortunately Harry touches a sandbag section of the wall but nothing happened.

"See, nothin' there" he says with triumph of self knowledge

But there isn't as Harry put it "nothin' there" because after a few hours, he develops a rash on his hand, and not long after blisters appear. He is sent off to the casualty station.

The troops are relieved of trench duties and they happily trudge their way through the warren of trenches back to the farmhouse in the dark, Tom is back on day to day duties again of moving ammunition and food and it is like this for all soldiers serving at the front. Four days in the trench then four days out, unless of course they are on a mission, which is usually carried out at night.

Later, Tom thinks about the two soldiers who were taken away. His regiment is debriefed and told that the Germans are using Yprite or mustard gas which doesn't kill immediately and has no smell. However, the effect on the air passages are quick, giving a feeling of not being able to breath as the gas burns the linings of the lungs. But the worst is to come after as the victims take days to die, and sometimes in stronger individuals, maybe a few weeks. Frank and Joe, they were such great mates and it seems to Tom that they'll never be coming back.

The whole of August is spent alternating between trench duties and moving supplies, with Cecil on his back constantly talking about how he'll get "those damn Boche". But now September is here and the rain eases off a bit, the ground dries a little although the occasional spell of rain keeps the ground muddy. After another sleepless night, the sun is rising and the troops are gathered for briefing, which means only one thing. Tom's platoon is going on a mission.

Chapter 7

The Reality of War

September 14th and three o'clock on this Friday morning, the platoon is getting ready to move out while Tom sits down to check his kit. Along with his rifle and bayonet is his haversack, in which is filled with mess tins, pouches of ammunition (170 rounds), water bottle, two grenades, shovel and entrenching tool. He closes up his haversack and undoes the top two buttons of his jacket and slips into his inside pocket a small first aid kit. He picks up three empty sandbags and tucks them into the back of his belt.

In the darkness the other men also gather their stuff for the march to their mission; Harry is back. His hand has healed, fortunately he didn't get very much gas residue. There are some scars on his hand but Tom can see that Harry uses his hand as if nothing had happened. Tom then notices some of the soldiers smearing mud on to their helmets.

"Why are you doing that?" he asks

"It's to dull the appearance of me 'at, make it difficult to see in any sort of light" says Bob

With that, Tom also takes his helmet off and smears mud onto his too, with Cecil copying the action. He put on his webbing, hangs his gas mask bag around his neck, slips on his rucksack and picks up his trusty Lee Enfield rifle and joins the platoon. When all the soldiers are lined up, the commanding officer shouts the move out command. Andy complains "what am I doing here?"

The soldiers march away in line with officers Knight, Addiscott and Bennett at the head.

The troops reach their destination, a German pillbox. The enemy is trying a new tactic away from the stalemate of trench warfare, bunkers made out of concrete that can withstand all but a direct hit. The St Julien-Poelcapelle Rd runs along back of German pillboxes. Sergeant Knight's platoon waits in shell holes and watches the pillbox in front of them. Tom, like the other men, has no idea what they are waiting for. He looks at his pocket watch, they have been here for an hour now and as far as he is aware, the Germans don't know the platoon is here. The sun is starting to come over the horizon when they hear a strange clanking sound and there down the road that ran behind the pillbox is a contraption of the likes no one have seen before, at least not working. They have seen tanks previously but only parked, and here is one making its way slowly up the road. The Germans are aware by now of its presence but can't get the machine gun round as it is fixed at the front, from where attacks are expected. They poke their heads out the back door and fire with their rifles at the mechanical beast, but the bullets just bounce off. The tank revolves its side gun on the round, points it towards the door and fire several shots. The bullets ricochet inside the pillbox, smoke pours out causing confusion amongst the Germans and while this is going on Bill creeps up on his own to the pillbox and hurls a mills bomb through the narrow opening of the concrete hideout. An explosion inside immediately sends the Tommies running towards the pillbox to greet the confused Germans who stagger out. The German soldiers that are still alive are rounded up and led away while the tank carries on its journey to the next pillbox.

A small team is sent back to inform command that the area is now secure along with the German prisoners. The pillbox now becomes a command centre away from home, and the officers immediately put the men to work as the entrance of the concrete housing faces towards the enemy and has to be made safe. Sandbags are placed at the entrance; the soldiers know that the enemy are not more than a few hundred metres away in their trench making them feel uneasy. Tom stands holding a sandbag while it is filled up with soggy earth, ties it and walks with it to the pillbox. Before he can get there he hears a recognisable sound, that of missiles. The Germans haven't wasted time in getting the information back to their headquarters and are shelling the area. The first shell hit the ground missing any soldier and explodes. Tom is standing with a sandbag in his hands when he hears that whistling sound he'd heard so many times before, but it is different this time. It sounds closer. There are no holes nearby to jump into then "PLOP". He stands there with his sandbag and slowly looks down. There is the shell at his feet, the top hasn't opened up so he knows it's not a gas bomb, it is an ordinary shell. It hasn't exploded and Toms' mind starts to race "what to do now?" he thinks. The answer comes from the soldiers in the pillbox.

"Run Tom" they shout, and keep shouting. He doesn't need any more encouragement, he runs as fast as is possible in the mud. The soldiers give him encouragement as he runs while shells explode all around. He reaches the door of the bunker and turns to look; two more men are behind him and running, it is Archie and Ed. Another shell lands right behind Archie and he is blown to pieces instantly, while Ed falls down screaming.

The soldiers stand by the doorway and look helplessly as Ed lay helplessly on the muddy ground, his face shows a grimace. Every time anyone as much as put their head near the door, a spray of bullets is unloaded by the Germans, which ricochet off the concrete walls.

"Lads, give me cover" says Tom.

Immediately the troops fire their rifles out of the doorway towards the direction of the enemy line. Tom dashes out of the door and runs towards Ed, grabs the loose folds in his jacket and pulls. The bullets make a 'slop' sound as they enter the mud. Much to the surprise of all around, the young lad also runs out and helps pull the body back in. The soldier is brought into the pillbox and is laid down on his front. The soldiers can see that the Ed's back has embedded into it pieces of shrapnel. Tom turns to Cecil "thanks Cecil, you did well"

Cecil raises his height a little with pride.

The men crowd into the bunker with little space to breathe, bullets whizz pass into the space above the men's' heads. The shelling stops but the guns are still firing, eventually even the Boche get bored of the continuous noise, and they too stop. The men stand around the edges while those in the middle manage to sit down. Bob stands with his helmet off.

"Put your helmet on" says Tom

"I don't want to" says Bob "it's hot and uncomfortable"

"If you get hit, you'll know about it"

The large man wipes his forehead then drops his helmet. He tries to pick it up but there are too many bodies crammed into the small space that he can't bend over. He finally gives up and tries to make himself as comfortable as possible.

"Try to get some sleep men" says the sergeant "and we'll try and get the rest of the sand bags done during the night"

The sun is starting to set while most of the men fall into a light uncomfortable sleep, they wake up at the least sound, then realise what it is and fall asleep again. Individuals take it in turn for sentry while others look after the wounded man who is lying on the floor amongst the legs and boots of the standing men. Ed gives out a moan every so often. Others try to get the sandbags up as quietly as possible and make the area as secure as they can, the odd bullet whizzes past their heads.

The sun starts to rise over the grey horizon, but before it can light up the sky properly, the hate bombardment begins again. The soldiers cower in the pillbox as the shells rain down. A shell hits the side of the bunker with such a force that the whole of the concrete structure moves, hurling men around men inside its walls. Chunks of concrete fly off in various places that hit the men's bodies. Bob tries desperately to find his helmet but can't reach down far enough. After the shelling has died down, there are cries of "is everyone alright?" Most suffer bruises on their arms and bodies. However, the large man lay propped up against the wall with a large blood wound on the side of his head. Bob hadn't heeded Toms' warning and dies from head injuries. The shelling stops altogether and the sergeant immediately gives the order to finish the sandbag wall. The soldiers carry out their orders while the odd enemy bullet flies past. Eventually the pillbox is made secure.

Ed is checked again but is found to have died from his injuries during the night. The soldiers try to console themselves with a brew but before they can even finish making the first cup of tea, there is a shout from Bill at the door.

"Sarge, the enemy are approaching"

The soldiers look out of the door over the sandbag wall and sure enough, there is a small troop of German soldiers walking their way slowly towards the pillbox. They are Stormtroopers, the elite of the German army.

Sergeant Knight says "alright, men! Formation!"

They wait for the Germans to get closer; they can see that two of the enemy are carrying different looking guns; containers are strapped to their backs. They let off a blast of their weapons that spray a jet of fire five metres long.

Charlie joins the small troop "Sarge, there's more round the sides approaching"

The sergeant pulls back his lips and says "right, I've had enough of this"

With that, he jumps over the sand bag wall and starts firing at the Germans.

Knight fires his rifle into the group while his troops watch in both fascination and horror. Tom rolls his eyes upwards and says "crikey, he's keen".

The soldiers get up and fire their guns. Sergeant Knight unfortunately falls into a shell hole full of mud, which isn't as dangerous as some he has come across but he still starts to sink and his rifle is out of his reach. He can get himself out of this one but some Germans have realised he is there and proceed to fire upon him. Knight withdraws his revolver and starts to fire upon the marauding German soldiers, killing several of them. In the meantime, his regiment are also firing upon the enemy. Tom has his rifle poised and fires shots upon Germans, killing several.

The sergeant uses all the bullets in his revolver; there is no time to work himself out of the hole as he has sunk further making it more difficult to get out, he has to reload. He pulls his bullets out of his pocket and opens the chamber. Just as he slams shut the chamber he looks up and there is a German soldier that looks down on him. The two men are at least five metres apart but the German has a clear shot and takes it. Sergeant Knight recoils in pain and slumps. The German is about to take a second shot when Tom, who is standing at least twenty or so metres away, can see what is happening. He raises his rifle and thinks back to his sharpshooting days at Hayling Island. He fires and the German soldier falls to the floor like a rag doll. He then charges and bayonets two soldiers. The Germans are on the run.

The Tommies shout at the fleeing enemy, rejoicing in their victory, unaware of what has happened to Sergeant

Knight. Tom slowly walks to the shell hole and peers in, fearing the worst.

"Well, don't just stand there, help me out soldier!" the sergeant bellows

Tom holds his hand out to Sergeant Knight and helps haul him out of the shell hole. But he has difficulty in pulling the man out; Andy and Bill come over and help. Slowly, the sergeant is pulled out of the mud. The sergeant stands up and brushes as much mud off while the two soldiers return to their duties.

"But Sarge, I saw you take a direct hit" stammers Tom

The sergeant brushes the mud off his revolver and replaces it in its holster. He then reaches inside his jacket, pulls out a silver cigarette case and throws it to Tom then walks off. Tom watches the sergeant walk off in disbelief; the man has just been shot and behaves as if nothing happened. He looks down at the cigarette case in his hand, he gives a quick laugh. Embedded into the case is a bullet.

A cry from Bill gives the realisation that the Germans weren't running at all; they just went to get a few extra men. The battle ensues but Tom is caught unaware as he is still holding the cigarette case, with his rifle on the floor. He turns round to see an enemy soldier with his container strapped to his back. The German is ready to let loose his fire of death; the men look at each other briefly but the neither see the young lad creeping up who fires his rifle at the German but misses. However the bullet pierces the cylinder the soldier is carrying that burst into flames. The man screams as he is engulfed in fire. Tom then picks up his gun and runs into the battle.

Finally, after much fighting, the Stormtroopers are finally beaten and their bodies lay strewn across the mud. Sergeant Knight tells the soldiers to wait around in a state of alertness while the support troops turn up. Tom and his young friend are given the duty of collecting the bodies of his comrades, so they first dig out the shell holes so that they form one long trench. The bodies are dragged to the edge of the trench and lay there. Tom goes from body to body and pulls off one of the dog tags, go through pockets and find personal effects to send back to family. He sees the huge body of Bob lying lifeless on the muddy floor; he pulls out a photograph of a young woman, presumably the wife or girlfriend. Tom thinks for a moment that Bob never mentioned he had anyone back home, but then the man rarely spoke unless he was addressed. The young lad holds a sandbag while Tom put in the personal effects, the bag is then labelled. The boots are taken off and kept for re-use, the bodies then rolled into the trench. Tom gives an extra thought for Archie who has no body to bury. With the soldiers buried, their rifles are pushed into the ground with the butt facing upwards, the helmets are placed on the butt and a label added to denote who the soldiers were. Tom stands there silent for a moment saying a silent prayer to his fallen comrades as the sun sets over the horizon and the relief troops turn up.

They have to wait for night fall before they can move out and return to base camp. Tom enjoys his meal that night, even though it is the same as the night before (and the night before), bully beef. The young lad can't stop talking about the events of the day and boasts about the fact they have seen off the Germans but the soldiers are just glad to be resting and carry on eating. Finally one soldier says to the boy "there are still thousands more of them out there for you".

Ellen stands waiting in a queue listening to the gossip.
"Food shortages? It's a disgrace"
"Yes, it's them Germans. They brought all this on us"
"Ooh, kill the lot of them, I say".
A woman tries to push in front of the gossiping ladies causing outrage to those people behind her, but she just receives shouting at her with physical abuse following.

A police officer is never far away from these queue sessions and he comes and breaks up the fight, the woman admits defeat and walks to the back of the queue. Ellen sighs with relief that the queue has returned to normal, she put her hand on her belly to reassure her unborn child.

Thursday September 20th at 5.40 am and the Post Office Rifles head down Shipstraat. There are some farms beyond St Julian, the farm they are after was Wurst Farm where the Germans have fortified. Since Tom has been here at Ypres, it has rained constantly throughout August and he has to be careful where he stepped. He's not sure what's more annoying, the rain or Cecil's incessant talking about how invincible the battalion is. The constant shelling from both sides has created large craters everywhere; the constant rain has filled them up. And he has seen what happened when something fell into the mud.

The troops sneak through the forest, or at least what is left of it. There is not much to hide behind; tree stumps are sticking out of the mud, with no other sign of life. Suddenly there is the sound of machine gun fire as soldiers all around fall, the ones who aren't hit scramble for the available tree stumps. Tom quickly dumps his haversack while he stands behind a large stump, turns and sees the young lad also standing behind a stump. Splinters fly into Toms' face as the bullets hit the dead wood, the young lad stands like a statue clutching his gun. He doesn't move and stares into open space as mud and wood splinters spray everywhere. He calls his name; the lad turns slowly and looks at him. There is a shell hole nearby, Tom points to it, the lad nods.

The machine gun rains its deadly death around Tom again and more of the tree stump splinters. He looks at the stump and thinks there won't be much of it left to hide behind. As the machine gun is firing at another part of the platoon, he makes a dash for it and as he runs past the lad, he grabs the boy's arm and pulls. The bullets make a splut-splut sound as they follow on the heels of the two men. Tom dives and drags the boy into the shell hole with him. The two bodies make a splash as they hit the side of the hole, any further down and they'll start to sink.

In the hole with them both is Charlie as mud flies everywhere and falls like rain into the hole.

"Sorry to gatecrash your party" says Tom

"You're welcome" Charlie replies "but we're a bit short on drinks"

Tom carefully looks over the edge; there is another shell hole further on. The boy also relieves himself of his haversack. A German soldier stands up from behind his sandbag wall and throws his stick grenade, which lands in the hole where the three soldiers are. Tom grabs the boy and pulls him as hard as he can; they both roll over in the mud to the next shell hole with the bullets following them again. In the shell hole is a tree stump which gives extra shelter from the bullets. Everything happens so fast that as Tom crouches down with his hands over his head, the grenade explodes, he realises Charlie didn't follow them. Mud and shrapnel rains down on the soldiers as they crouch in that hole. Tom sits up and wails "he didn't move"

In the shell hole is Bill who is looking around the tree stump.

Tom says "careful, you'll get shot".

"No kidding" says the soldier, "I need to see where the gunner is"

Bill takes a second look as a crack is heard and splinters fly. His gun is hit and unfortunately his hand is holding the gun. He takes a sharp intake of breathe and holds up his hand, his middle finger is missing and blood is pouring out.

Lance-corporal Addiscott stands up and shouts "you soldiers, forward", he continues rallying the men when he gets peppered by machine gun fire and falls to the ground. Tom is tying a bandage round the Bill's hand and tells him "we ought to get you some first aid".

The injured man replies "no, we've got to go forward".

As he says this, the sergeant runs past.

"Sarge" shouts Tom, but his shouts go unheeded "here we go again"

Too late, Sergeant Knight has run towards the German gunner. The gunner sees him and swings his machine gun round to face the oncoming Tommy but he's not quick enough, the sergeant rams his bayonet into the German who then falls away from the gun. The second German tries to grab the machine gun but he too gets bayoneted. A third German picks up his gun and points, but Sergeant Knight was a little bit quicker and shoots the soldier dead. The troops are inspired and rush out of their shell holes and fire at the other German soldiers, the enemy runs off leaving the area to the victorious Post Office Rifles.

The area has been secured but with both Lance-corporals dead, the soldiers carry on clearing up the mess and some soldiers enter the pillbox. Sergeant Knight sends two soldiers back to base camp (one of them being Bill), while the rest of the platoon fill up their sandbags and create a wall around the farmhouse. Some of the soldiers stand behind the sandbag wall with their guns ready.

The Germans are retreating slowly, walking backwards towards a small trench. Behind them is a machine gun, which can't fire as it will cut down their own men. The German soldiers turn and run towards their trench, only three survive long enough to jump in. The machine gunner lets rip mowing the British Tommies down as they advance. Sergeant Knight again rushes as the gunner tries to pull the gun around. His colleague pulls up his rifle, aims and fires. Knight let out a yelp as the bullet tears through his shin, but through the pain he carries on running Before the German can fire again, he receives the shaft of Sergeant Knights' steel blade through his heart. Knight quickly turns on the gunner who now can't turn his machine round far enough, and hits the man with the butt of his rifle before shooting him dead. He stands there at the top of the trench looking in.

The process of fortifying the new position begins in earnest. As soon as the sandbag wall has been made, Tom calls his sergeant over.

"There" he says

"Where?"

"That hole. I saw something move"

"Saw what move?"

"That hole over there"

They edge their way to the edge of the hole. The other men join them at their side. The Tommies peer over the edge of the large shell hole with their rifles ready. At the bottom are three German soldiers sitting in the mud with their hands up, with terrified looks on their faces. Around are their dead comrades. The British shelling has done its job, pulverizing the enemy into submission. Cecil brings up his rifle and fires, just missing the nearest German. Tom and another soldier grab the gun, pull it away and ask "what are you doing?"

"Well they're Germans aren't they?" the young soldier replies.

It is at this point that Tom looks at the German cowering in their trench that he has pity on them. He realises for the first time that these German monsters are just men, just like himself he thinks, and that they too have families back home with mothers and wives waiting for them to return. Here they are frightened and at their wits end, just as many of the British soldiers have been during Toms' stay here in Belgium. They are following orders just the same as Tom is. And just like him, they are patriotic to their country but don't want to go killing other men, wherever they come from.

"These men are prisoners of war, and need to be taken back to camp" says Tom

The boy reluctantly agrees despite his chance of going home with stories of how he killed the enemy.

The German trio climb out of the trench and stand with their hands up. A photograph is on the floor, one of the Germans goes to pick it up.

"Stop where you are!" shouts Andy with his rifle pointing to the face of the German, who quickly resumes his hands up position. Tom, still holding his rifle at the ready, bends down to pick up the photo. It is a picture of an attractive looking woman. He looks at it, and then offers it to the German.

"Your wife?" he says as the frightened looking soldier just stands there. Tom moves forward to shove the photo in the pocket of the captured man and then he puts his hand on his breast pocket as he remembers his own wife.

"Danke" says the German soldier

The pockets of the German soldiers are searched and all documents handed over to the Sergeant, who has finally succumbed to his wound and sits down. He has by now applied a bandage to his leg and is holding it on to stem the bleeding.

"Some of you take these prisoners back, and somebody give them a cigarette or something"

Harry gives each of the three men a cigarette and lighter.

Tom jumps into the trench, the smell almost unbearable as the bodies of the dead soldiers are starting to decay. He sees in the mud a book; he picks it up and wipes the mud off. 'Mit Jesus in der Feld" a German prayer book with same picture of Jesus looking over a soldier as in English version. He puts the book in his pocket, a souvenir.

Just then, a troop of soldiers march in.

Sergeant Knight bellows "where have you been? You're a bit late"

The young lad chips in "yeah, you've missed all the fun"

The leading man walks over to the Sergeant and says "you're the commanding officer of this platoon"

"Yes"

"You're to report back to base"

The troops, tired and worn out, get themselves together to move out and leave the new platoon to secure the area. Two soldiers put Sergeant Knight on a stretcher,

"That's a Blighty one you got there Sarge"

Despite the humour, the troops are down, the platoon much smaller now than when it first came to this area, about twenty men.

The only way through the quagmire is to walk on duckboards. Sometimes they are broken or missing from shelling. It is impossible to see because using a light would attract unwanted attention. Suddenly one of the platoon falls off a broken section of duck-board. It's Andy and he sinks into the mud waist deep as other men drop their rifles; a small group surround them with their rifles at the ready. Tom reaches his hand out to the soldier "grab my hand"

Andy replies "it's alright Tom. I'm alright"

He says again "grab my hand"

"No, it's alright Tom. Dying isn't so bad you know. I'll be in a better place"

Tom tries desperately to plea with the man who has been through the worst anyone can go through, but he isn't as strong as the other men and just feels like giving up

"Damn it man! Every soldier is needed here; we all depend on each other"

The soldier looks up at Tom with pathetic sorry eyes "bye Tom"

"Come on, don't give up on us. Don't give up on yourself"

Tom's hand remains outstretched.

"Come on"

Sergeant Knight can't get up but says "you give up now Beal and we all might as well go home, so get yourself up here now! That's an order!"

Tom makes a small extra stretching movement with his hand "come on now"

Andy is by now up to his neck in mud. The other soldiers are now cheering him on "Come on man"

"We've got to get a cup of tea"

"There's a tin of bully beef with your name on"

The soldier lifts a heavy mud laden arm up to Tom, the two men clasp hands. Tom pulls and pulls but the soldier wasn't budging. One of the German prisoners kneels down beside Tom and grabs the man's arm. The two pull and slowly, the soldier moves upwards slightly. They keep pulling until the soldier was far enough out for another prisoner to grab and pull, then others are able to grab any part of the uniform and pull. Finally, Andy is out and lying on the duck-board covered in mud and everyone who pulled is exhausted.

"Right" says the sergeant "pull out"

The stretcher bearers pick up their sergeant and the troop walk.

The platoon march back to camp, weary and hungry, desperately needing proper sleep. Tom has only been here two months, but it feels like years and he is by now hardened like the other soldiers who have been here long before him. He looks about him as he marches towards the camp; the landscape is barren, devoid of plant life. The only clue that a forest had been here are the tree stumps sticking out of the mud. Every now and then, a hand or foot sticks out of the mud. Tom knows these individuals will be lost as there is little chance of retrieving the bodies. Over there is a half submerged tank, one of its tracks had come off and sticks up in the air. The soldiers are too tired to hate the Germans now; besides, they have now seen the enemy face to face. They are not like the monsters they were told about before they joined the army. Many men question the war, religion and most of all, the people at the top who sent them here in the first place. The hatred they have for the German soldiers is not as great as when they first came to the Front and they look at their prisoners like they had all suffered a common foe. Like the other men in the troop, Tom wants to go home.

CHAPTER 8

THE BIG ONE

"24TH SEPTEMBER 1917

Dearest Ellen,

Monday morning, the start of a new week. I have a little time to write you a letter; we have been so busy here. It must have been what, a month since I last wrote. At the moment, I am doing service duties that just involve moving rations about, keeps us busy you know. I am overjoyed to hear we are having a child, I hope it's a boy.

We have had a week of some sun and the ground is starting to dry out, but today is pouring with rain again and I am stuck inside this tent. Eventually I will have to go out with the rest of the lads to move rations, probably in the rain. We have captured many German outposts and have seen the enemy off. I have finished my spell of trench duties yesterday and happy to be away from the Front. Still, the shells keep me awake at night so I am very tired. The work keeps me occupied but it is very quiet (in relation to how it normally is you understand) so I think we must be getting close to finishing this war.

I have had a proper wash and shave, not just a quick once over in the dugout. I feel very clean at this moment in time. It's nice not to be covered in lice, they itch like mad. I am relieved I'm not fighting at the moment although I'm told the Germans are on the run. We should defeat them and I should be home very soon, I miss you so much. I love you and can't wait to be back home again.

Your loving husband

Tom"

Ellen puts the letter down and sighs; she runs a hand over her belly. Ellen's' mother is also at the house, she moves closer and also put her hand on the belly to feel the baby moving inside. She is concerned that the baby will grow up without a father; she senses that her daughter feels the same too. She knows so many women who have lost husbands and sons.

"Tom says he should be home soon" says Ellen
"I hope so, Love"

Tom tries to sleep but the noise of the shells is incredible, mud flies over him and pieces of shrapnel fall into the trench. Eventually the noise stops but Tom still can't sleep the anticipation of the noise starting again plays on his mind and he spends the entire night drifting in and out of half sleep. Soon dawn comes round and the shelling starts again. Eventually, the shelling stops and the soldiers are pulled out of the trench for mundane duties although this morning there is nothing mundane about these duties. All about are broken carts and dead animals. Occasionally, the hooves of mules stick up through the mud, or a piece of mule is found on the ground in amongst pieces of machinery. Tom carries out his duties the best he can until a cry from a soldier, he and others run to the stiff erect man with his hand over his mouth and his eyes tightly closed. Poking out from the mud is a face, a soldier from who knows which side, had been hit by a shell, killed then covered with mud; no one knows what else was buried in the mud. The officers come and order the men back to work while a small team come to find out who the soldier was and to deal with the body.

But relief from the drudgery can't come too soon; the platoon is moved to a camp near Poperinge for rest. The troops are in a large house with washing facilities; Tom takes his jacket off and a mass of black objects fall out onto to the tiled floor, the tiny dots then scurry off in different directions. There are more of them on Tom's shirt, crawling around; he quickly brushes them off onto the floor.

"So these are lice, are they?" he says

"Hey Tom, don't lose them. They'll keep you company when you go over the top" says Andy

"How do you know we're going over the top?"

"We haven't done so far, it's got to happen soon"

"Yes, I mean, why do you think we're having this rest period? They're cleaning us up for our final charge" says Harry

After his wash he is having a shave and he is relishing every last moment of this shave, each stroke is a joy. Tom thinks it was strange really that something so mundane, something normally taken for granted is so cherished at moments like this. Other men are also in the room standing over their respective washbasins having their own joyous time whilst shaving, although they have shaved over the past month, it was a quick once over that still left patches of stubble. Other men are washing, but the feeling of being clean after so many months of dirt and grime is wonderful. Some men are outside the house brushing of dried and caked dirt although Tom has already done this and he has his jacket hanging up waiting to be put on again especially now it was clean of lice.

The young lad is also standing over his washbasin having a shave and it is obvious to the other men that this lad has never used a razor before. There isn't even any point as he has no hair on his face, but he tries and as he slides the blade across his face, he cuts himself.

"Ow!" he cries in pain.

"Look lad" says Tom "don't bother. Just have your wash and get dressed"

He washes the soap of his face, pats it dry with a towel and walks out with his jacket, looking despondent.

"He can't be more than sixteen" says Tom

"Or seventeen" says Andy

"Doesn't matter' he shouldn't be here. He's too young"

The soldiers are now clean, very unusual out here, and the soldiers have been given a days leave. The group decide to visit Poperinghe town centre where many soldiers from other regiments go. There is a house there that serves good food and most of all, BEER! Tom and the chaps have managed to cadge a lift on the back of a supply truck, which stops outside Talbot House that the soldiers refer to as Toc H and walk in.

"Who's getting the drinks then?" asks Tom

"Uh-uh" says Andy as he wags his finger, "you play the piano"

"We-ell...alright!" he says very excited.

That is all the encouragement he needs, and sits down at the piano and plays while Harry and Andy get the drinks. Other soldiers in the room start to gain interest as Tom plays tunes that most of the people there recognise and it isn't long before the crowd gather around the piano and sing along. Despite the occasional bomb explosion in the distance, people ignore the battle, which is the furthest thing from their attention right now. They are going to have a good time.

Eleven o'clock and the house starts to clear out. Not so Tom and his group who order food. The men pay for their food and Tom is just about to pay for his when man behind the bar put his hand up.

"No mate, you get your food for free" he says in an English accent "you played well tonight, entertainment makes people buy more beer" he taps his nose with his finger

"My name's Tubby Clayton" he says and offers an outstretched hand. Tom takes it and shakes the owner's hand.

"Thank you" he says "it's what I do best"

"Right, you go and sit down, someone will bring your food over to you"

Tom sits down; his colleagues pat him on the shoulders. The bar is emptying out now; Tom thinks there will be plenty of sore heads tomorrow morning when the sergeants are bellowing for early drill. The food comes over, the serving woman says to Tom "you lovely soldier, I like your playing"

She makes a piano playing motion with her fingers then turns and walks off.

"Eh Tom? You played well tonight"

"Too right" he says "I haven't lost it"

The group carry on eating until they are finally thrown out at midnight, now they have to make their way back to camp. The men are drunk but in control of themselves, not so the young lad who can hardly stand up. He has to be supported by the other soldiers before he finally falls unconscious.

Tom and his fellow revellers wake up in the morning because of loud shouting from the sergeant.

"Get up you lazy sods!" he bellows.

The men get up, wash, shave and go to the breakfast table where the men sit down.

"Ooh, my head" complains Cecil

"Can't you take your drink then?" says Andy

"Well, it must have been strong stuff" the young lad complains

"Taah! It was normal beer, and you only had two pints. I saw you"

"Yeah, you don't normally drink, do you lad?" says Harry

The boy pulls his plate closer and gulps his food down while the soldiers chuckle to themselves.

"Ere, it seems strange us doing all this work out here" says Andy

"But we always move rations on occasions" replies Harry

Tom carries on eating but listening to the conversation.

"No, there's something else. I dunno, lots of activity" Andy keeps the conversation going

"What kind of activity?"

"Well, higher ranks walking around, you know, stuff like that"

"Doesn't mean anything"

"And all the drilling, and what about out rifle cleaning? We've done that for two days in a row"

"That's just normal for when we're not on trench duty"

"No, I tell you, something's going on"

"What though?"

Tom finally pipes up "perhaps we're going over the top"

Despite the men realise what he has said is true, there are still gasps of disbelief "no!"

"Yes, that's it, they're preparing to go into battle, I mean the BIG battle"

The boy stops eating abruptly and looks around at the faces of the men at the table.

"'Yes that's right, I hear rumours that they want to take Passchendaele" says Andy

"And all these battles we've been having, they're just little ones to clear the way for the main battle" says Harry

The men can't be sure, it's just gossip. After breakfast, as the men carry on working, there is a meeting in the farmhouse, the sergeant comes out and calls his men together.

"Tomorrow" says the sergeant "we attack at dawn"

This is the big one they are told, the big push to gain the town of Passchendaele. The POR are to be in reserve while the main regiments start the attack. The soldiers break up and continue with their work with a heavy weight on their shoulders, the rest of the day is spent moving and loading rations as usual. During the night, Tom gets little sleep but not just because of the nightly bombardment. This is the big one, they are sure. He thinks of Ellen, wondering what she is doing now.

Ellen stands on her front door. She looks to her right and sees the neighbour a few doors down the road, both women are sweeping the front porch as per usual every morning. A post-lady approaches the neighbour and hands a brown envelope. She opens the letter and reads it then she burst into tears and howls. Other women who are also outside, they rush to her side to comfort her. She sobs loudly, Ellen holds her head down. She looks up again as the post-lady walks towards her, holding a brown envelope. Ellen can see the 'OHMS' printed on the envelope. The post-lady stops by Ellen, looks at the envelope then walks on. Ellen watches the post-lady walk off, has a quick look at the sobbing neighbour, then holds her head low and walks back indoors.

Wednesday September 26th at 5.40 am, the troops have been awake for half an hour now. Battle order is commanded; the men hand in their heavy rucksacks and greatcoats, having only a small rucksack. Handed out are two days rations, extra ammunition and bombs, picks or shovels. A thick mist hangs in the air, the view obstructed to little more than five metres. The soldiers are told to line up in a queue then the commanding officer says "two minutes". The first person passes it on the chap behind, who then passes it behind and so on, the message passing down the line. The message gets to the young lad who can't speak, Tom says to the man behind "two minutes" and the message carries on. He leaned forward and notices the boy crying. He says quietly in the boys ear "don't worry, we'll get through this"

The boy replies "I'm not really Cecil, I'm Cedric and I'm only seventeen"

"Oh" says Tom

"I used my dead brother's birth certificate. I wished I hadn't"

"It's a bit late to be declaring that now"

"If I die, tell people who I am. I want my parents to know".

"Yes, I'll do that, don't you worry about that"

The men line up and wait. The British guns fire their arsenal continuously for about an hour, with retaliation from the enemy then the British guns stop and there is an eerie silence. With so much noise going on for weeks, here is something that the troops haven't heard for a while.

Tom leans back slightly and says to Harry behind "hear that?"

The soldier looks puzzled and says "don't hear nothing"

"Precisely"

The Germans start to send shells over again but they are up to something more deadly. In between firing normal explosive shells they are also firing gas shells, no one hears the plop as they land and let out their deadly cargo. No one is aware of the smell as the gunpowder constantly going off everywhere masks the smell. No one knows about the gas they are about to run into.

As the soldiers line up to go over the top, they are standing with their tin cups while waiting for the rum to be dished out. The CO walks down the line with a large earthenware jug and is pouring into the men's cups which they gulp down in one go.

"Ah, here comes the old grey hen" comments Andy.

The young lad stands and looks into his cup while Tom gulps his ration down "aaah!" then passes his mug over his shoulder. The soldier behind takes the mug and hangs it on Tom's haversack.

After Tom has his rum he leans forward and says to the lad "drink up your grog, lad".

The boy gingerly drinks the contents of his mug and gasps, his mouth is on fire. Both Tom and Andy in front of the boy both smile. Tom holds his hand over the boys shoulder takes the mug and hooks in onto the boys' haversack.

Waiting for the time is like eternity, all the soldiers know what is going to happen and some (like Andy) can't control their emotions anymore and just cry. Then the commanding officer turns to the first man in line 'one minute'. That minute seems like an hour but the time does come, and the line marches through the catacombs that are the trenches. The first line trench is now empty of the first and second lines and fills with the reserves. A message at one end of the line that says 'bayonets'. As the first man inserts his bayonet onto the end of his Lee Enfield, the next man does the same, and the next and the next. The copycat action is so quick that the whole platoon fixes their bayonets within a few seconds. Tom stands there with his gun, stands and waits. Then the whistle blows and the men climb the ladders and over the top.

The soldiers go over; they run across the empty area between the two sides' trenches totally unaware of what the gas that has been released; the Germans in their masks fire a few shots at the oncoming Tommies. The German machine gunners also in gas masks let rip with their guns, the British soldiers stand little chance. Many are mown down from gunfire.

Nothing can be seen further than a few metres but there is something eerie about the place. Tom looks about him while he is running, there is no-one. An occasional 'plop-plop' of bullets hitting the mud and maybe a bullet would whizz past. Then he notices, soldiers lying on the ground, some still moving with their hands at their throats. A carpet of soldiers litter the ground, all of them are down. No one is allowed to stop to see to the wounded, he has to keep running, let the stretcher bearers deal with these men. He realises that this can't just be gunfire, he starts to choke.

"Ohno" he thinks "gas. I've breathed it in, it's too late".

He drops his gun and grabs his throat, and then coughing fits begin. He stumbles and falls to the ground himself.

Tom lay in the mud gasping for air but can't breathe, he sees his fellow soldiers also falling to the ground and over there is Cecil with his hands at his throat, choking. There are bullets flying overhead that go ignored, there is just the inability to breathe. He can just make out blurred images, his sight gets worse as the burning takes hold, with heavy tears flowing to try and combat the searing effect of the gas. "This is it" he thinks, perhaps never to see the end of the war. The last thought passes through Tom's mind is whether he will see Ellen again.

The final reserve troops are ready to go out into No Mans Land when the order comes to ring the bell and put on gas masks, which the soldiers do with perfection having performed the operation hundreds of times before. They are ready; they climb the ladders and walk quickly out into the mist, fired upon by the few remaining German gunners left. Many men fall with bullet wounds, but enough get through to the enemy trench to take it. The allies are a step closer to taking Passchendaele.

But while the battle ensues, Tom lays there in the mud. Everything is blurred because the tears flow so much, it obscures his vision. As he lay there gasping, he doesn't notice that his watch and picture of Ellen slide out of his pocket and onto the muddy floor before he slips into unconsciousness.

CHAPTER 9

A BLIGHTY ONE

THE BRITISH FINALLY SUCCEED IN capturing the German trench but at a cost, hundreds of soldiers lay on the ground. The mist hangs in the air still; Tom is barely conscious and is aware of people around.

"There's another one here still alive" comes the unknown muffled voice.

Another man joins the first; they are wearing gas masks and rubber gloves. They lift Tom onto a stretcher leaving his father's watch and the picture of Ellen in the mud. The stretcher bearers start to make a move, the rear bearer's boot treads on the watch and picture, pushing them into the mud then the two men carry him across the battle area. Although Tom can hardly breathe, he can still see. Just. His eyes are sore with unbelievable pain and everything is out of focus, but he can make out the bodies lying everywhere before he passes into unconsciousness.

Several soldiers are carried into a concrete bunker, a field hospital at St Jean. The soldiers are laid out on tables and the doctors and nurses are wearing gas masks, rubber aprons and rubber gloves. Tom is starting to regain consciousness just as water is poured into his eyes; he is unable to breathe properly but gives out a strangled scream. He tries to sit up but the doctors hold him down. The nurses are stripping him of clothes and as soon as he is naked, another nurse comes in with a bucket and starts to scrub his bare skin; the other patients in the room receive the same treatment. Tom is panicking now and his breathing becomes harder and more erratic as he fights for breathe. His skin itches and his eyes hurt, he can't see properly as his eyes are streaming, everything is blurred.

Tom fights for breath and for consciousness; he is desperate to know where he is and what happened. The nurse lays a clean sheet over him, he tries to speak but all that comes out is a strangled gasp. His lungs are burning, his throat is on fire, and he is gasping for air. He feels like he is underwater and has swallowed in liquid, it feels like he is drowning but he can still breathe. But only just. His itchy skin isn't even registered in his mind as his main concern is to get air into his lungs then panic starts to set in again but he unable to do anything about it as he slips into unconsciousness.

Tom doesn't know what the time or day is but he is aware that time has passed as he slowly awakes, he is also aware he is somewhere different. He has been transferred to Poperinge Hospital. He is still finding it difficult to breathe but can't see at all now. Suddenly nurses come into the room; they're not wearing protective clothing this time but go through the same routine as before. Water in the eyes and a thorough wash. The soldier in the next bed is also being washed, it is the young lad. The boy gasps then is quiet. The nurse stands back and says to Matron "he's dead". Nurses flock to him but there is nothing more they can do, the gas has taken its toll. Tom can only hear the chatter as doctors and nurses attend to the wounded.

The dead soldier is carried out while two nurses attend to Tom's body wounds. Although he has been cleaned several times since being brought into hospital, he still has to have treatment. The first nurse pulls back the blanket and Toms' chest is covered in reddened blotches, looking rather like scarlet fever. By his left armpit is an extremely large blister, with several more scattered around his body. The nurse goes through the same routine of washing the skin of gas residue, while the second nurse inserts a hypodermic needle into the large blister and draws out the liquid. The needle is re-inserted for the next blister, and a third until all the blisters had been evacuated, the blisters are then covered with dry sterile dressings.

Tom can feel his eyes were swollen, and indeed they are. The nurse pulls back the swollen eyelids and pours a saline solution into Tom's eyes, causing a near panic. He hates this but tries his best to allow the liquid to penetrate onto the eyeballs and run off into a clean dressing. All needles and used dressings are taken away, even at this stage no chances are to be taken as the gas can still be soaked into the flesh.

"I can't see" croaks Tom, still gasping for breath.

"Calm down Private, you'll be alright" comes the reply from the doctor.

"But I can't see!" is the last thing Tom says as he burst into a coughing fit. Every now and then he coughs up blood as the gas has burnt the linings of his lungs. Many men die not from the gas itself, but from asphyxiation from liquid in the lungs.

While Tom is being treated, back in Britain Ellen is outside in the early morning September sunshine with no idea of her husband's whereabouts. The post lady turns up at the gate, hands a brown envelope to Ellen and she sees the OHMS stamped in the corner. The post woman walks off leaving Ellen just standing there looking aimlessly at the envelope, afraid to open it. She let go of the broom handle and let it drop to the floor. She walks inside and her mother asks "what is it dear?", and then notices the letter in her daughters' hand. Ellen finally opens the letter and reads it; she falls into her chair with her mother looking concerned.

"It's a military form, he's alive" she finally says, "but he's injured, been gassed".

"So he should be home soon then?" asks Mrs Bushnell as she takes the letter from her daughter.

"I don't know, it doesn't say. It doesn't even say where he is"

A few more days pass and Tom feels much better but he still can't breathe properly. He asks the nurse "what happened to me?"

The nurse replies "you've been gassed. You're in Poperinge Hospital, they're going to ship you back to England"

"How long have I been here?

"Oh, you've been here five days"

"Will I die too?" asks Tom weakly.

All the nurse can do is to look him in the eye then walk away, but Tom not being able to see is unaware of the answer.

"Nurse?" he says into empty space.

Also in the same room are other soldiers who lay in beds in the field hospital all waiting to transport to England. An officer comes in and shouts "right, load them up on the train". Orderlies pick up the stretchers as the officer shouts "you lucky bastards are going home".

Tom wakes up coughing and spluttering, then gasping for breath, slowly the coughing fits die down to a gasping. He is lying in a bed and realises from the movement he is on board a ship presumably he is on his way back to England. He hears a voice shout "ey up lads, it's the white cliffs of Dover"

There are murmurs of joy amongst the patients, some of whom try to get up, sit up or lift their heads up just to get a glimpse of those white cliffs. For most of them, this is home. No going back to that forsaken battlefield, now it is the green fields of England. Tom thinks momentarily of his local pub and warm beer, he still can't see but is aware of that fresh sea smell which helps him to forget about the odour of gunpowder and decaying mud.

The ship enters dock at Dover and Tom is stretchered to a waiting ambulance where he is transferred to a train that goes to Eastbourne station, where he and fellow soldiers are carried out on stretchers off the train to waiting ambulances. A crowd of people have gathered at the station and now watch the soldiers being carried out, someone starts clapping which spreads to the rest of the crowd. Tom is aware that something is going on but isn't sure exactly what, the crowd pat the soldiers as they are carried through. He is loaded onto an ambulance which then drives to Summerdown Hospital with other convalescing soldiers.

In the ward there are many soldiers who had suffered horrific injuries; some have no legs or one of their arms missing. The nurses are young women who joined the VADS and have never seen such injuries before. They stand and cry before matron comes and tells them to get on with their work. Tom has been made to sit up with large pillows behind his head but he is tired. He is aware he is near the sea because he can smell the salty air, and he can hear the seagulls in the distance. He coughs a few times before falling asleep.

He sleeps soundly but later in the night come the dreams, he is back at Passchendaele and running for his life. He turns round to look at the men following him, a whistle then an explosion. The men are blown to bits. Tom sits up quickly in the dark, awakening with a stifled scream. He breathes quickly and deeply, sweat is dripping down his forehead. He quickly calms and slows his breathing down. The sun is rising and shines through the gap in the curtains when a nurse comes and opens them to allow the full sun light to come. Tom can see light, nothing is distinguishable but at least he can see something.

"Ah, Mister Lane" says the nurse "you're awake. The doctor will see you soon"

She walks off, Tom unaware that she has gone, turns to the empty air and says "what's happened to me?"

No reply "hello?"

A voice from across the ward "hello"

"Who's that?"

"I'm Fred; I got hit by a shell. Lost me leg, like"

A northerner, thinks Tom.

"I'm Tom. I'm sorry, I can't see you"

"I thought as much. You've been gassed, haven't you?"

The doctor walks in "ah, Mister Lane"

"Huh?" Tom is suddenly aware the man is next to him.

"What happened to me?" he asks.

"Well" says the doctor "you were in the middle of a gas attack and you've received quite severe injuries"

"Will I die?"

"Can't say for certain...."

"The others die, the ones I saw before, they died"

"Well it's too early to say. Because you have deep lungs, that's what probably saved your life"

"I can't see"

"That's due to your eyelids being swollen. They'll settle down and you should regain your sight soon"

He asks the doctor "excuse me, but do you know how the battle went?"

The doctor isn't a military man and replies "I don't know where you fought but I'll find out for you"

Later an officer comes into the room.

"You're Private Lane aren't you?" he says

"Yes I am"

"I hear you play piano quite well"

"I do, or at least I did. Sorry sir, but I was at Passchendaele and wondered what happened to the outcome of the battle"

"Let me see now, you were in the 58th Division"

"The Post Office Rifles, Sir"

"Quite. Ah, you were attacking the trenches at Gravenstafel"

"Yes"

"Your regiment successfully took the trench"

"Will I be going back?"

"Ooh no private. The British troops have been pulled out; it's down to the Canadians now. However, once you have recovered then you'll have to go back to duty"

"Great, I'll be a C3"

The officer replies "you'll still be providing for the war effort, you won't be totally useless. They'll find something for you to do"

Tom thinks for a moment and then says "thank you, Sir"

"If there is anything else I can do for you, don't hesitate to ask"

"Yes Sir, thank you Sir" Tom thinks for a moment again then says "a cup of tea would be nice"

The officer replies "quite so, I'll see to it on my way out"

Tom listens to the echo of the footsteps making their way out of the old room. He sits there thinking for a while. Usually soldiers go back to the Front once they are well but the idea briefly pops into his head that he may not get well at all. He quickly dismisses any further thoughts before it is too late and the idea sticks.

Tom soon makes friends with Fred who hobbles over on his crutches.

"Could you write a letter for me please, it's to my wife"

"Of course I could" a quick rustle of paper "alright, go ahead"

"Dearest Ellen..."

"That's her name is it? That's a nice name like"

"Thank you"

"Dearest Ellen,

I am in Summerdown Hospital in Eastbourne. I have been injured but not seriously, I was gassed and have a little cough but I am quite alright and am doing really well. I am temporarily blinded which is why the writing on this letter isn't mine. I had to dictate it. We won our battle but I will be out of action for a short time while I get better.

It would give me great joy if you could visit me.

Please come.

You loving husband Tom"

Ellen looks at the letter with a tear in her eye. She put the letter down on her belly and runs her hand over her lump. She immediately picks up pen and paper and starts to write as her mother comes in.

"Hello Love" she says

"Hello Mother. I have a letter from Tom"

"Oh how is he?"

"He says that he's alright. I'm just about to write a letter back"

Tom lay in bed when a nurse came around with this morning's letters.

"One for you Tom" she says as she hands the letter over. Tom tears it open and feels the paper. Fred comes over and asks if him if he wants the letter read out.

"Yes, go ahead"

119

"My Dearest Husband,

I cannot come to see you as I am into my ninth month of pregnancy. I can walk around and do the housework but the stress of a long journey will bring on the birth prematurely. I am glad to hear you are back in England and I am thinking of you. Mother sends her regards.

I hope you are well and make a speedy recovery.

Your loving wife, Ellen"

"Aah, you're having a kid" says Fred in his northern accent

"I know, isn't it lovely?"

"Now if that isn't something worth getting better for?"

Several days have passed since the doctor told Tom of his injuries. The swelling on his eyelids has diminished significantly and Tom can make out images now, albeit blurred. A further few weeks pass; Tom is still lying in bed but he can get up and walk around although he has to stop frequently to catch his breathe. His vision is much improved and can now make out peoples faces. Reading fine print in the newspapers is still a difficulty though. He has received several letters from Ellen and she has promised to visit as soon as she can after having the baby.

A doctor comes in and asks Tom how he is doing. He replies that he is alright but gets tired easily.

The doctor replies "That's understandable. You had quite an amount of toxic gas, although I'm told, a fair amount of it dispersed by the time you got to it. However, I have something to tell you. You may have survived a gas attack and few people do that this far, but your lungs will have suffered terrible burns and it is possible you may have permanent damage"

"How long will I live?" asks Tom

"That is difficult to say. These are new injuries to us, relatively so, as this is a new gas the Germans are using. You may have a short life or you could live for years. However, you won't be able to do any kind of active work"

After his evening meal, Tom settles down to bed. He still tires quickly and like the other soldiers here, gets bored. There is little to do but talk to each other, there is no entertainment. Only earlier today a boy found a grass snake in the garden, captured it in a glass jar and brought it inside. He tied it to the leg of his bed until a nurse came to check him she saw the snake and screamed. Matron came in an ordered the boy to remove the snake but the rest of the ward laughed till it hurt them.

Tom finally slips into a late afternoon sleep, but is quickly woken up by the soldier across the ward who starts to gasp for breathe, then shouts and screams. He gets out of bed waving his arms, staggers a few steps before some nurses come to calm him down. He shouts obscenities both to the world in general and to the nurses then finally, the nurses calm the man down and put him back to bed. Tom can't sleep now; he gets up, puts his dressing gown on and wanders. He has to stop every now and then to hold onto something while he gets his breathe back, and then he continues.

Tom walks slowly around the main room until he sees a small room off to the side. He walks inside and stops to look around the room; it is some sort of games room with a piano in the corner. He lifts up the lid and looks down at the white and black keys for a while before he taps a key. He listens to the tone as it dies away. He taps another key, then another and before long a tune appears. Inspired by his memory he sits down and plays, feeling the keys and getting into the swing of it. It isn't long before another patient comes in after hearing music, then another. Very soon, most of the patients now join the throng that is standing behind Tom. One man starts to sing, and then the others join in. At last, here is the entertainment the men have been longing for.

Tom sits by the window looking out into the November garden. It has been a light drizzle of rain for a week now and the sky looks so grey and miserable. He looks out impassively, having no feelings at all was better than being miserable. How any one can stand being in those trenches for years was incomprehensible to Tom, he was in them for two months and that was unbearable. He feels a twinge of guilt for not being there for his comrades, and pain for those who died. Thousands of them, slaughtered. Suddenly someone runs in.

"Have you heard?" he shouts with joy to no one in particular, while holding aloft a newspaper.

"No, do tell us dear boy" comes a sarcastic reply.

"The Canadians have captured Passchendaele"

Now people are interested and start to sit up. The young man unfolds the newspaper and sits down while everyone else crowds round to read the article.

"We've won the war"

"That's it lads, we've won. The Germans have to give up now"

"Don't be so sure" Tom says to himself "they said before it would be over by Christmas"

But no one can hear Tom from the other side of the room; he just let them get on with their jubilation.

Monday, 12th December and another letter from Ellen;

"Dearest Tom,

Last Tuesday I have had the baby, a little girl. I've called her Ivy"

Tom Looked up "Ivy, her name is Ivy" he continued reading

"I am suffering from exhaustion and so won't be down for a while. However, here is a Christmas present to keep you going"

Tom looked down and opened the parcel. He pulled out a jar of jam. He laughed.

"...it's home made jam, I hope you like it. Mother made it"

He put down the letter "a little girl" he says

Fred overhears him "you got a kid?"

"Oh yes, a little girl, Ivy"

"Ooh, that's grand like"

It's the new year of 1918; Tom is sitting by his bed reading. They had a reasonable Christmas there in the ward, but most of all, he misses his wife. But joy comes to him this particular morning when Ellen walks pushing a pram.

"Hello Tom" she says

Tom jumps up and throws his arms around her, and then he starts to choke.

Ellen is worried "are you alright?"

Tom sits back down, wheezes then says "I'm fine, it's just the gas. I'm alright really"

Once he gets his breathe back he asks "who's that?"

"Meet your new daughter" Ellen picks her up from the pram

"Our daughter?" replies Tom

"Yes. This is little Ivy"

"Ivy" Tom has to catch his breathe "it's a lovely name".

Ellen asks how Tom is; he replied "I'm alright….sort of. I'm afraid I will be ill for quite a while".

Suddenly, the soldier across the room starts to yell and throw his arms around. Ellen watches, feeling the fear rise up inside her; she clasps the baby closer to her. Nurses come in and calm the man down. She looks slowly round the room; there are men with no legs, men with bandages covering their faces, men with an arm missing. The realisation hits her that this is the effects of war and that men don't just die. Some live with horrible injuries.

"You alright?" she asks Tom

"Yes, I'm fine" Tom thinks it would be a good idea not to let Ellen know the full severity of his injuries.

"You haven't got anything missing, have you?"

"No, nothing missing. I'm all there" he pulls up his pyjama legs and twirls his feet.

Ellen looks relieved then says "your father's well. He's made a full recovery"

Tom smiles "that's great"

They spend the rest of the afternoon talking, not saying much as Tom got out of breathe too quick but he doesn't mind, for now, this is the best moment ever. For the first time since the gassing, he felt things are looking up.

CHAPTER 10

WAR'S OVER

1918

MARCH; TOM IS SITTING BY the French windows with the doors open; It is still cold, the winter being a bad one. Some birds are starting to come out even though there are few leaves on the tress and bushes. He listens to the birds quite intently; these are sounds he hadn't heard for a while. In fact, he has never paid attention to bird song before and he realises how beautiful the noise is. He thinks it rotten that this is something positive to come out of the war, which he thinks, is still going on and those men are suffering. He wants to be angry inside but he can't as the bird song soothes him, he loves the twitter of whatever it was in the bush. Perhaps now he has time on his hands he can learn the types of birds.

A nurse comes over.

"Mister Lane, aren't you cold by the window? Here let me close the door"

Tom put up an arm "no, I'm all right, really I am"

"Well, if you want to catch your death of cold..."

"No, I'm fine. It's soothing to be by the window"

A doctor comes over with a clipboard

"Ah, Mister Lane. Diagnosis shows that you are well enough to go home"

"Really?"

"Yes. But you must be careful. Your lungs are still in a poor state, you need to keep in touch with your doctor but you're all clear to go home"

"When do I leave?"

"Tomorrow"

Tom gets dressed in a suit provided for him although it's not quite the perfect fit but it will do. Or is it that his body has changed? He was always thin but now he seems different, he looks at himself in the full length mirror. He smoothes the creases in the jacket, then steps closer to have a look at his face. He seems older. Much older than the nearly twenty eight he is, looks more like thirty eight. He steps back and runs his hands down the lapels of his jacket but stops when he gets to his breast pocket. He puts his hand there and tries to feel for something then realises that neither the watch nor the picture of Ellen are there.

He picks up his small suitcase also provided for him although he doesn't have much to take home. He walks into the ward and says his goodbyes to everyone.

"Goodbye Tom" they say

Tom replies back with a goodbye.

Fred says "you keep in touch like. I'll hobble your way soon"

"Yes, you look after your self Fred"

"And you make sure that little Ivy grows up fine"

"Yes I will thank you"

He walks out the door with a cough or two. Walking away from the hospital front, he turns and looks at the old building.

"I hope you all get better" he says to himself, then turns and walks.

Ellen is waiting on the platform of Waterloo station while the engine slowly pulls in and stops with a squeal. Steam fills the air but she can see the doors opening and people getting out of the carriages. She holds up the letter she received from Tom telling her that he will be coming home today. A guard walks along closing doors that are left open then blows his whistle, the train starts puffing and slowly pulls out of the station. More steam stills fills the air even though the platform has been cleared of passengers, she hangs her head. Suddenly from somewhere in the steam cloud, she hears a cough, then some wheezing, she looks up and a shadowy figure is standing there. The steam has started to clear a bit and figure becomes more recognisable. It's Tom! She runs towards him and throws her arms around his neck at which point he starts wheezing and coughing.

"Tom, are you alright?"

He calms down then says "yes, I'm fine. Couldn't be better"

She looks at him and says nothing

"Come on then, I'm dying for a cup of tea" he says

He picks up his suitcase and they walk off together to catch the train to Queens Park.

Off the train at Queens Park both walk out of the station but further down the road Tom has to stop and put his suitcase down on the floor.

"What's up love?"

He wheezes "The suitcase gets a bit heavy after a while. I'll be alright in a bit"

Ellen picks up the suitcase and carries it "come on soldier"

An older man walks in the opposite direction and turns to Tom and says "you heartless beast, letting a woman carry heavy items. You should be carrying it for her"

Before Tom can speak Ellen quickly butt in "do you mind? My Tom is the victim of a gas attack. He's a war hero"

The chap gave a cough and a mumbled "sorry" before moving on.

They walk past the butchers which was empty. The window has been boarded up.

"Oh, so the butchers have moved out" notices Tom

"Yes, they moved away" replies Ellen. They both walk slowly on.

Tom sits at the kitchen table while Ellen is cooking the dinner.

"Hey, it's nice to be home again" he says, he is still a bit wheezy.

"Are you sure you're alright? I mean you still have that chesty cough" she replies. As she draws the roast out of the oven, she put two house bricks in.

"Oh I'm fine" he says although he is sure Ellen isn't convinced. "It's just a cold, I'll be right as rain soon, you see"

They sit down to eat.

"Ooh, you don't know how good this tastes to me. Months of bully beef and jam, then hospital food...." he inserts a mouthful of food "...mmm!"

They carry on eating in silence, Ellen wants to ask what happened at the Front but daren't.

Tom eventually says "they want me to go for a medical next week to see if I'm fit to return"

Ellen put her cutlery down quickly "what, the army?"

"Yes, they'll put me back on duty"

"They're going to send you back to France?"

He wants to correct her. It isn't France, it's Belgium. But he thinks never mind, most people refer to the entire Front as France.

"No, I won't be going back to the Front. I won't be fit enough; they'll just put me on some light duties. I signed up and it was for four years"

Disheartened, Ellen picks up her cutlery and carries on eating.

After dinner the bricks are brought out of the oven and wrapped in cloth. Each brick is put in each side of the bed to warm it up, because although it is March, the cold winter is still here. The two sit in chairs opposite each other.

"Where's Ivy then?" asks Tom

"She's with my mother. She'll be round tomorrow morning"

"You know, I could do with a swift half"

"Tom! You are not going down the pub! Not in your condition"

"I know, I won't go down. But there are certain things I have missed"

"Yes, like beer. I think you should stay home more often, help me with Ivy"

"I'd like to see my friends though; I should imagine there's not many of them left"

"You should see your parents; I think they've missed you"

"What, me sour old mother!"

"Tom! She's your mother!"

"I know, I only jest. I certainly have to see how my father's doing"

"Oh yes, he's doing well. You'd never have thought he was gassed looking at him"

"And to think, I got it worse..."

Tom stops.

"Yes, it would be nice to see the family"

It isn't long before he does go down the pub to see what few friends are left.

"Those Germans should be made to pay" says Patrick

"What they did makes me sick" continues Arthur

"Yeah, too right. Bayonetting babies and all that" says Fred

Tom cut in "excuse me, but they are people just like us"

"What, are you mad? They took us to war" replies a near angry Arthur

"Yes, and they destroyed lives. They're monsters!" says Patrick

Tom replies to their accusations "I saw Germans out there in Flanders. Of course the people at the top started the war, but the average soldiers were just like us. They were shot at like us, they had families like us, they were blown to bits like us and they certainly didn't bayonet babies. They had no control over the war. We were just puppets for the leaders to play with. I'm sure those soldiers will be suffering in the same way as the soldiers over here. They are just people".

"You're not on their side are you?" demands Arthur

"Yes, you sticking up for the enemy?" continues Patrick

"Nooo! I'm just saying that those soldiers had to fight in the same way we did. I'm proud I fought for my country, don't get me wrong. I'm glad I went over there.....but the carnage. So many people were slaughtered on both sides, needlessly"

"Ye-es" urges Fred

"Look, if you looked into the eyes of a dead man, I'm sure you would be affected by it, whoever they were. I saw those Germans and they were scared like us. They just wanted to go home like us. And like us, they saw their comrades blown to smithereens"

"Sorry Tom"

"Many more men will die before the guns fall silent, and at this rate it'll probably go on for another few years, it's totally pointless"

The group sit thoughtful for a moment. Fred pipes up "I'll be glad when this war is over"

"Amen to that" and they all raises their glasses and take a gulp of their beer.

"Here, can you still play the piano?" asks Fred

"Of course" Tom replies. And with that he goes over to the piano, lifts up the lid, sits down and plays. Within a few bars, people crowd round and start to sing.

The next month, Tom has returned to army duties but is now down at Regents Park. The area has been converted to a depot with large military tents on the grass. He walks around with his clipboard checking supplies; a lot of the men here are from the Front with minor injuries including Bill with his missing finger. With injuries just like himself although, he thinks, there's nothing minor about being gassed or shot. Still, these are injuries that aren't life threatening but the men with them would not be fit enough to fight, and would even be a danger to their comrades. Tom can hear the birds in the aviary at London Zoo, it was pleasant. He feels good at being home but at the same time, feels a twinge of guilt of not being there to help out his mates. Still, as the officer in the hospital said, he is still helping the war effort.

It is a fine sunny morning but a little chilly. He gets the usual bus to work and picks up his clipboard and stops when he notices the headline in the newspaper that is lying on a table. All he sees is the word 'Passchendaele'. He picks up the newspaper and can't believe his eyes. He goes to say something but just slumps into the nearby chair. He is gasping and wheezing, other soldiers rush to him.

"Tom, what's the matter?" asks Bill

"Slow down, ease your breathing...that's it... slowly now"

The soldiers eventually calm him down although he looks close to tears but doesn't cry.

"Now...what's up" asks Bill

Tom points to the newspaper; the soldier picks it up and reads the headline. He turns the newspaper round for all to see.

"Germans take Passchendaele" Bill reads out the headline

"What was it all for?" Tom eventually speaks "I mean, why did we get our injuries if it was all for nothing?"

"Easy Tom" reassures Bill

"I got gassed at Passchendaele, for what? And they let the Germans take it back?"

He grabs the newspaper and throws it on the floor. The soldiers mill around until an officer comes in "come on you lot, back to work"

The soldiers saunter off and Tom slowly gets up and picks up his clipboard, with a heavy weight on his shoulders. The officer can sympathize with him but everyone has a job to do.

November the eleventh, Armistice Day and the news spread that the war has ended. The streets are filled with joyous people. Someone knocks at the door, "are you coming out then Tom?"

"No" he replies "I'd rather stay in"

He closes the door and walks back in. "what's the matter Tom?" asks Ellen "don't you want to celebrate?"

"No" he says

"But the war's ended; I thought you would be pleased?"

"No I'm not"

"But..?"

He looks at his wife and says "how many people have died? Too many that's what. If you had seen the things I have seen, then you wouldn't be celebrating either".

"Sorry Tom, but I can't understand what you went through. You don't ever talk about it"

Chapter 11

The Epidemic

1919

The New Year and the winter is cold again; a flu epidemic hits the country. Tom goes round to see his parents and his mother lets him in.

"Your father's ill" she says as soon as he walks in "he's got flu"

But he doesn't listen and goes straight upstairs as fast he can manage to the bedroom.

"He won't want to be disturbed" shouts mother from the bottom of the stairs.

He walks into the bedroom and sees his father there lying in bed, it reminds him of that day in Beaversbrook. Tom senior looks up "Hello son" he croaks

"Hello father. How are you doing?"

"Alright" he said although Tom knew that he wasn't, the flu had killed many people already over the country.

"After all we've been through at the Front" wheezes father "we have to succumb to this"

"I'm sure you'll get better, you did it before"

The two men sit in silence. Tom coughs. His father turns his head and wheezes "you need to be careful son. In your condition you do not want to get the flu"

"Sorry father, but I worry about you"

"Don't be silly. I've got my family; you need to see your little girl grow up"

Another silence.

"She's rather a sweet little girl. She looks like Ellen, you know" says father

Mother comes in with some hot tea.

"I think it's time for you to go son" wheezes Tom senior.

Tom stands up and walks to the door.

"I'll pop in again tomorrow father" then he walks out.

But Tom doesn't see his father the next day because he himself has been exposed to the flu virus. He is in bed feeling sorry for himself while Ellen called the doctor out who examines Tom. He wraps up his stethoscope and turns to Ellen as he put his instruments into his case.

"Keep him indoors, don't let him go to work and make him drink plenty of water"

The doctor leaves the house while Tom wheezes. Ellen sits down next to the bed and watches her husband gasp for air while he turns his head slightly and looks up at her. All she can do is lay a hand on Tom's shoulder to reassure him.

Mrs Bushnell is at home in Kensington and bounces Ivy up and down on her knees.

"Whee!"

The little girl giggles. Mrs Bushnell stops and sits in silence.

"Your Mummy will be here soon, don't worry, it's just that she can't leave your Daddy alone"

Ivy gurgles.

"Your Daddy will get better you know"

The baby turns her head towards her Grandmother and gives a toothless grin.

"I hope he'll get better" she says

Ivy gives a scream and waves her arms around.

"Alright, here we go"

She bounces the baby up and down on her knees.

"Whee!"

A week passes and the doctor is at Tom's side again holding the sick man's wrist.

"Hmm, seems like a healthy pulse to me"

Tom coughs.

"So, I'm fit and healthy again"

The doctor gently put Tom's hand down.

"Not by a long way. Your chest sounds like it still has a lot of stuff to get rid off, but that could be your war wound"

The doctor slips his stethoscope in his bag.

"I'd stay in bed for a while longer if I were you. You're not ready to go back to work yet"

"But I can go down the pub then?" says Tom with a grin

"You stay in bed for another few days at least"

He turns to walk out of the room and looks at Ellen

"Good day Mrs Lane"

"Good day doctor, and thank you"

The doctor goes and Ellen walks over to Tom, bends over and then tucks in a sheet.

"How's my father, have you heard anything?" Tom asks

"He's fine" replies Ellen with such assurance in her voice "he's up and about, fit as a fiddle"

"Good old Father, he never gives up, does he?"

Tom is bored being stuck in bed all day so he gets up and staggers to the piano where he plays a little, the March sunshine beams through the windows. He stops playing for a bit, listens the birds singing then plays some more. Ellen walks into the room, she is coughing a bit. Tom stops and turns on the stool towards her.

"You know, I'd love to get back into the big band stuff, I really miss it"

"You get better first before you start thinking about things like that"

"Yes, the big band sound"

He carries on playing the piano while Ellen carries on coughing. Tom stops playing.

"Are you alright?" he asks

"I'm fine, just a little chest infection. I'll be right as rain in a few days time"

Both Toms survive and are better or at least to the condition they were at before they caught the flu. However, Tom senior seems to retain a little of the symptoms and although he goes back to work, he can never fully recover. Tom has spent two weeks off work but is now fit enough to go back to work at the depot at Regents Park where he works until Wednesday May 7th, when he is himself discharged from the army to return to work at the Post Office. The army has sent the relevant letters to the Postmaster and all the paperwork has been sorted out.

He gets ready for work, pins his medals to his postal uniform jacket and an hour later he walks into the sorting office, albeit slowly, down the gap in between the crowd of postal workers who are mainly old or very young. There were a few men who had been in the war and return relatively unscathed but not many, he is one of the few. The main difference Tom notices though was there are more women postal workers. Occasionally, a man takes Tom's hand and shakes it. He sees Bill there too.

"Welcome back Tom"

A few murmurs round the back of the crowd "yes, welcome back"

He gets to the end and the Postmaster is standing there with a sack.

"Welcome back, Tom. I hear you had quite a time at the Front" and he hands Tom his sack of letters.

At first he tries delivering letters but a two hour delivery takes five hours as he has to constantly rest. His breathing won't allow him to walk far before he has to sit down. On this particular day the sun is shining Tom sits down on a low wall wheezing with his hands by his sides on the wall. He feels something on his hand and looks down, it is a Labrador that looks at Tom with big brown sad eyes, one of the dogs he used feed before he went away and the dog remembered Tom.

"Sorry mate, I haven't any chocolate for you" he says as he strokes the dog's head.

"Well, I have to go. See you"

He gets up and walks down the road, wheezing. The dog's eyes follow him and he can see that Tom isn't at all well and gives a whimper.

At the sorting office the main sorting area is nearly empty of postal delivery people, there are a few people milling around sorting letters. The Postmaster comes out of his office "where's Lane?"

Everyone nods their heads.

"He's been gone five hours" looking at his wrist watch.

He turns to walk back into his office when one of the sorters calls him back and as he turns, Tom walks into the main room with his empty sack gasping for breath.

"Tom? Are you alright?"

Tom sits down and gasps "yes…I'm fine"

The Postmaster isn't convinced but walks off and leaves Tom sitting there gasping for breath.

Tom walks home that takes over an hour, a journey which normally takes twenty minutes. He opens the door of his home, hangs his jacket up and drops into his armchair where he falls asleep. At five o'clock, Ellen wakes him up for dinner. Ruby Baker who lives above Ellen's mother was there looking after young Ivy while Ellen cooks. She picks up the baby and put her in her high chair, Ruby is now sixteen and often helps out with the baby when she has finished work. Ivy has a wooden clothes peg in her hand and is chewing it but Ruby gently pulls the peg away while Ivy giggles and waves her arms around. Ellen dishes up the food and turns to Ruby and says "you can go now Ruby. Thanks for your help"

The young girl puts on her coat "alright Mrs Lane. Bye Mr Lane" and with that, she is gone.

Tom sits at the table and says to Ellen as she put the dinner plates down "I must get some chocolate"

"Oh! For me?"

"No, for the dogs on my round. I didn't have any for the Labrador today"

Ellen looks slightly disappointed. After dinner, Tom falls asleep in the armchair again.

At 8 o'clock, he wakes up and put his coat on and walks, although very slowly, to the pub. There he drinks with some old mates, the rest not coming back from the war.

"Tom!" shouts someone across the not so crowded bar room.

"Over here"

As Tom walks over, he can see the man standing by the piano.

"Come on Tom, give us a tune"

He doesn't need much encouragement and sits down and plays without getting breathless doing this, he has plenty of energy for it. It isn't long before people gather round for a sing-along along with half pints of beer for the piano player.

The next day Tom goes to work. He is late again and as he walks into the sorting office wheezing, he is called into the office.

The Postmaster says "Tom, someone has gone out on your round"

"What?"

"Sorry, but it cannot be not noticed that you are finding it a strain to complete your round on time. I'm afraid I have no choice but to put you on sorting duties"

"But I like my post round"

"I know, but we need to get those letters out, and you er... find it difficult to keep up. Go to bin 42 and help out there"

Tom, looking down, can't argue. He does find it difficult to walk the round, he is only twenty nine, a young man but an old man of fifty can out walk him now. He slowly gets up and walks out of the office and quietly closes the door behind him.

Tom sits at home watching Ruby play with Ivy. The baby keeps putting a peg in her mouth and Ruby pulls it out.

"Don't eat that, it's dirty"

The baby just giggles. Ruby is good with little Ivy, and it gives Ellen some breathing space.

"Don't you mind looking after the baby?" asks Tom

"No not at all"

"But don't you work as well? Aren't you tired when you get home?"

"No it's all right. I enjoy looking after her. It's fun"

"What do you do...For work?"

"Oh, I'm a cashier. I work for Harrods"

"Oh very posh" says Tom

Ellen overhears and says "now now Tom. It's a very good job, with good prospects"

"No no, I know I'm pulling her leg and so on, but it's good, isn't it?"

"What Mister Lane?" asks Ruby

"Well, when I went away, there weren't many jobs for women. Now I'm back, everywhere I go, I find women in the work place"

Ellen isn't sure if Tom is serious or not but she changes the subject and mentions the butchers.

"What butchers?" asks Tom

"You know, the one that got smashed up"

"Oh yes, the piano"

"That's the one. Well, they're still there"

Tom looks slightly puzzled then asks "they didn't go away?"

"No, they stayed here"

"Don't people bother them now?"

"No, the crafty so and so's changed their name. The butchers is called Jones now"

Tom just smiles.

1920

Tom is happy he still has a job; many soldiers returned home to find that they are unemployable and he is grateful for this job despite it not quite being what he wants. He enjoyed being a postman before but thankful for small mercies. However he finds it difficult to walk to work and get there on time and he doesn't want to lose employment, he has to get up a lot earlier just to make sure he is on time, he had thought about a possible solution for a long time. He is well paid and saved hard for quite a while so that he can put down a deposit for a car. He buys one, a Model T Ford, cheap in comparison to other cars but still beyond the reach of most people.

He pulls up outside his house, this mechanical thing that clanks and roars. Ellen comes out to see what the noise is. No one stops outside in a car, not here anyway.

"Tom, what is that?" she says. Ruby is standing further back as young Ivy peers out from behind her. Tom is standing admiring the car.

"It's a motor car, so I can get to work"

Ellen says "do you know how to drive it?"

"I've got my licence, what more do I need?"

He stands there with his thumbs in his waistcoat pockets. He turns to Ellen "come on, let's go for a ride"

"In that?" she says pointing

Tom bends over and turns the handle, the engine kicks back and the handle flies out of his hand.

"Bit temperamental these things" he says. He tries again and the engine roars into life. He climbs in and motions to Ellen "come on"

She climbs in apprehensively while Tom puts the car in gear with a crunch, and pulls away. Ruby manages to hear Ellen say "look after Ivy, Ruby" as the car speeds away into the distance. They drive up to the end of Malvern then turn right and drive around the block.

"There, what do you need to know to drive a car, eh?"

Down south then into the Harrow Road where Ellen slumps down further into the seat.

"Trams use this road" she wails. She starts to wheeze and cough uncontrollably.

"Does the car bother you?"

"Yes" she says

The car clanks and grinds and only when they pull up outside their house does Ellen relax. She climbs out as the engine stops with a splutter and she goes straight inside while Tom sits in the now silent car holding the steering wheel with pride. He need never be late for work again.

143

Also on Tom's mind is his music and he wants to get the band back together. He contacts the few people who are still alive and starts his first rehearsal, although he had played a few times since the war with hastily put together army bands. Tom wheezes and gasps for air, the other chaps wondering if Tom can make it through the session. Once they start playing, he keeps it up, the band members are happy and decide now is the time to start looking for shows.

It doesn't take long, Tom finds a gig and the show goes well, he is excited about this and can't stop talking about it.

"Time to look for another show" he says

"But Tom, aren't you married? With a child?" one of the band members asks

"Yes" he replies calmly "I can still pursue my love of music"

Tom comes home from work to find the doctor in the house.

"What's going on?" is all Tom can say

Ellen is laid out in the armchair with a blanket over her.

"Your wife has a chest infection, she should be well soon. Just keep her warm and plenty of fluids"

"How is she now?" asks Tom

"She'll need looking after, just make sure you can attend to her needs. She'll be too tired to do anything on her own"

"Tch, I wanted to go down the pub tonight"

The doctor looks over his glasses at Tom "no, you need to stay in tonight. She needs you".

1922

New Year, the end of January and over three years since the end of the war. It is a cold, snowy day when there is a knock on the door, it is Uncle Albert.

"Tom, come quick, it's your father"

Tom put on his jacket and walks as fast as he could to keep up with Uncle although he can't keep up and has to stop to catch his breathe. He carries but Uncle Albert by this time has disappeared into the house even though it is only about fifty metres away. Finally, Tom reaches his parents house, the door is open and he goes in. There is no sound but his own wheezing. He climbs up the stairs to the first floor bedroom where some family members are, there is Uncle Albert, Liz, Ada and mother. He sees his father lying in bed very still and he realises his father has died. He slumps down in the nearest chair and quietly says to himself "goodnight son.....goodnight father".

Tom doesn't have much time to mourn as he spends a lot of it looking after Ellen; his mother-in-law is round a lot also helping out. His wife still has her chest infection so at the request of her mother Tom takes her down to Dorset in the summer. They drive down there to a quiet Bed and Breakfast. They go for short walks which make Ellen perk up a bit although Tom can't quite keep up with her but is able to breathe alright, he feels better than before. The fresh air and slower pace of life really helps with his health. However he can't cope with the quiet.

"I want to go home" he says

"But we haven't been here long"

"I know but I'm bored"

Too much peace and quiet doesn't provide enough stimulation for Tom so the next day, they drive back. Mrs Bushnell is looking after Ivy and keeps the flat clean, when the door opens and in step Ellen and Tom.

"What are you two doing back so early?" she asks with a slight irritation in her voice.

"Oh, Tom. He couldn't stand the quiet"

Ellen's mother becomes more irate "what do you mean couldn't stand the quiet? What about Ellen? This was for her benefit"

"Mother, it's all right. I agreed to come back home"

"It's not all right!" and she picks up the nearest object which happens to be Tom's banjo. She swings the instrument round and hit Tom on the back of his head.

"Fresh air is what she needed"

Ellen quickly moves in between the two as Tom starts to wheeze.

"Stop it mother!" she says.

Mrs Bushnell retreats and tosses the banjo on to Tom's armchair, she put her coat on and says "I'm going"

The door slams as Tom picks up the banjo and slumps into his armchair. He massages the back of his sore head as Ellen brings in a damp cloth to sooth the bruise.

"Hmm, not sure if you deserved that. I'll have to think about it"

"Sorry love, perhaps we should have stayed there" he says.

"Don't worry about it now; we'll go down the pub later on, shall we?"

"What about Ivy" they looks at their daughter who had been oblivious to the whole affair as she is busy chewing wooden peg.

"Your mother can look after her... come on Ivy, give me that peg, you're a bit old to be chewing that"

"Peg" says Ivy with her arms outstretched

"You know" says Tom "she's always chewing those pegs"

"Yes?"

"Well, we should have called her Peggy"

Both laugh.

Tom has another show. It went well and afterwards he talks about the prospect of stardom.

"Sorry to dampen your spirits old man" says the trombone player "but music hall isn't the in thing at the moment"

"Oh, what are you talking about man? They loved us"

"Did you not notice? The hall was only filled to half capacity. It seems people don't want to come out any more"

The banjo player adds "yes, that's true. We have to compete with that new jazz craze"

"Nonsense" says a slightly irate Tom "they can't drink in the auditorium any more. That stupid law banned drinking alcohol during the show. Once the punters get over that, they'll be back in their hundreds"

The saxophone player decides it was his turn "look Tom, why should people come out to see a band when they can hear it on the radio"

"Without coming out of their house"

"And they can have a glass of beer while they listen"

The men sit around in silence holding their respective instruments. Eventually the trombone player pipes up "I for one cannot play regularly..."

"What.....?" Tom stands up

"Listen old chap, I have a family. I can't leave them on their own"

The banjo player adds "I'm a family man too, Tom"

Tom turns to the drummer "and you?"

"I'm afraid I too have a wife"

"We're not young men any more Tom, it's hard work playing in a band, I need time to spend with my family"

"But" says Tom trying to reason with the band "we can make a career out of it. We'll be well off"

The men just shake their heads.

"Sorry Tom, we're not pulling in the crowds anymore"

"That's right; we just can't do it with families"

"We don't mind the odd show here and there but not all the time"

The band walks out one by one with their instruments. As the drummer walks out he turns and says to Tom "you could always join a jazz band"

Tom goes white and clenches his fists. The drummer decides it isn't wise to stay and quickly leaves. Tom sits there in the back stage room on his own.

"Jazz? How can he say that?"

He put his head in his hands; his dream of becoming a well known band player was not to be.

Another day at work completed and Tom pulls up outside his house. He can't park in his normal spot as there is another car there. He recognises it as being the doctor's car. He quickly parks up and jumps out; he rushes up the stairs as fast as his lungs could carry him.

He walks into the kitchen.

"Ellen?" he asks but there is no one there.

He looks in the living room but no one is there either. He goes up the stairs to the next floor and walks into the bedroom and there is the doctor standing over Ellen. Alongside them is Mrs Bushnell.

"What's going on? Is she alright?"

The doctor turns round "she has a chest infection"

Ellen coughs and turns her head to look at Tom.

"Hello Tom" she croaks then coughs.

"Hello Ellen, are you alright?"

He turns to the doctor "is she going to be alright?"

The doctor pushes his stethoscope into his bag "she should be fine, just keep her warm"

"She seems to have a lot of chest infections; it's not the flu is it? We had that flu three years ago and she never caught it then"

Tom is worried.

"She just has a chest infection, keep her in bed until she gets well"

The doctor leaves.

"Thank you doctor" says Mrs Bushnell

Tom sits by his wife "are you alright?"

She replies "I'll be fine, don't you worry"

There are muted voices in the background as the doctor and Mrs Bushnell are talking. She enters the room.

"She's ill you know" is all she could say

"Mother?" Ellen croaks

"If you had stayed down in Dorset, she would have been well by now"

"Mother, don't blame Tom"

"Sssh, calm yourself down" says Tom

Mrs Bushnell put her coat on "you'll be alright now?"

"Yes mother, I'll be fine, if you could just look after Ivy for me"

Mother takes Ivy by her hand and walks out with her.

"I'll be in tomorrow... and you" she turns to Tom "no going down the pub tonight, alright?"

Tom just nods. Mrs Bushnell leaves with Tom and Ellen alone together.

1923

January, the night is cold and the snow has lain but not very thick. Tom is asleep and dreaming, he is in Flanders again in the trenches. Shells are going off all around them, dirt flies in the air and fall on him as he ducks and covers his head with his arms. A machine lets rip and the bullets ram themselves into the corrugated iron trench wall, leaving a line of holes.

"That was a close one, I might not have been going home" he says to his comrade. He turns round to the man he is talking to and recoils in horror to find the man has no head, just a hole where his head should be and blood spurting out. Tom wakes up and sits bolt upright, sweat is pouring down his forehead. Ellen stirs.

"Tom, are you alright?"

Tom is panting now "yes, I-I'm fine"

"Are you having another of your nightmares?"

"Yes. But I'm alright now"

He drops his head onto his pillow while Ellen drifts back to sleep.

Ellen is getting worse with her illness and spends many days sitting in her armchair with a blanket over her; she has been diagnosed with tuberculosis and feels so cold. When she leaves work for the evening then Ruby looks after Ivy, who is now nicknamed Peggy. Tom comes home from work on the 15th of January. He is his usual wheezing self but on this day he walks through the door and there are people in the house. His brothers-in-law Ralph and Frank, Mrs Bushnell, his mother and his sisters Liz and Ada. Ruby is holding Ivy.

"What's going on here?" he asks.

"Tom, sit down", says Frank.

"Why? What's going on?", then he realises. It was Ellen.

"The doctor did all he could, she went peacefully"

Tom sits down, breathing heavily and gasps for air. Most people would have found it difficult, but Toms gassed lungs can hardly cope with the pain. The room is filled with standing quiet people, except for Ellen's sobbing mother.

CHAPTER 12

IS THERE MORE TO LIFE THAN THIS?

ELLEN IS BURIED IN PADDINGTON cemetery and Tom weeps as the coffin is lowered, he feels so low. Normally a cheery chap, it is too much for him now. After the service he leaves the weeping crowd of people, and walks, and walks, it took him hours but he reaches the canal. There he slumps onto the grassy bank and sits with his head in his hands, wheezing.

"This life..." he says to himself

He looks up; there is the boatman with his horse pulling the coal boat.

"Hello young Tom"

But he just wants to be on his own, so he gets up and ran, he manages to reach the bridge before he slumps on to a stone wall. He gasps, he wheezes and splutters.

"Yes, take me" he says

After what seems like hours to Tom but is only minutes, he calms down. His breathing slows down and he walks off.

Tom finally gets home at midnight. Ivy isn't there; she is being looked after by Mrs Bushnell and he just sits there in the dim light in an empty house. He sobs until he falls asleep in his armchair. The next morning he wakes up with a start as he hears the door open and Mrs Bushnell is standing there holding Ivy.

"Shouldn't you be at work?" she says "and where were you last night?"

He jumps up and quickly rushes to his bedroom where he changes into his postal uniform.

Everyone notices at work that Tom is not a happy man; his clothes look as though they had been slept in and he is unshaven. They try to console him but he is too much down in the dumps, it had been too much even for a cheery chap like Tom. He needs to speak to someone but there isn't anyone. His father is gone and mother is a misery. Mrs Bushnell herself has locked herself away in grief except when she comes round to the housework at his place. He gets through his day the best he can and goes home, he isn't hungry and after sitting in his chair for an hour, he goes to bed.

He tries to sleep, although for hours upon hours he is in that twilight state, not quite asleep but not quite awake. He tosses and turns and eventually, he falls into a deep sleep. He dreams, this time he isn't sure where he is, it looks like No Mans Land. He stands on a piece of solid ground that is wet, surrounding him is mud but he holds his Lee Enfield in ready pose with the bayonet attached. From the darkness appears Tommies all around him who are in various states of injury, they are from his old platoon. Bill with his missing finger, Big Bob with a lump of concrete in his head and blood pours down his face; Charlie is totally covered in blood. Other Tommies are there too, some with an arm missing, some with their chest peppered with bullet holes.

They hold out what arms they have and walk slowly towards him.

"Help us Tom" moans Charlie.

"Yes, help us" says Harry

He drops his gun.

"Please, leave me alone" he wails

"Help us Tom, help us"

As the Tommies walk forward, their legs start to sink into the mud.

"Help us"

The arms are almost within reach of Tom so he tries to move back but behind are more arms. He tries desperately to find a way out but he is surrounded by wailing Tommies.

"Help us"

They sink slowly into the mud.

"Help us"

Their faces disappear into the mud leaving their arms above the surface. Eventually, everything sinks away, leaving Tom alone again. He is panting. He looks all around and sees no one or anything.

"Please, I want to go home" he says meekly "I want to go home"

Suddenly, a hand pops out of the ground and grabs Tom's leg, it pulls hard and he starts to panic. Then another hand, and another, and another. Several hands have now got Tom by the legs and start to pull him down. He is sinking into the mud himself, which starts to bubble with water.

"Help"

He is down to his waist now.

"Ellen, help me!"

He is down to his chest now.

"ELLEN" he shouts just as his face is about to disappear below the mud.

"ELLEN" he sits bolt upright in his bed. He looks to his left but the bed is empty, sweat is dripping down his forehead.

"Ellen?" he whispers

His hand pats the empty side of the bed. He pulls back the covers and gets up. He switches the light on, puts on his dressing gown and walks down to the kitchen. He goes straight to the sink, turns on the tap and splashes water on his face. He looks up, straight into the mirror at himself; he is appalled by the state of his aged skin. He pats his face dry with a towel and goes back upstairs. He takes his dressing gown off and turns the light off. As he sits down on the bed, he stops.

"Gran'pa" he says to himself "I'll go see Gran'pa"

On his way home he pops in to see Grandpa William, he pulls up in his car outside his Grandfather's home.

"Tom!" says Grandfather "come in, young lad, come in"

"Thank you Grandfather, although I don't feel so young"

"If you were fifty years old, you'd still be young compared to me"

"Sorry, I just feel a bit glum"

"Losing Ellen?"

"Yes. And father"

"Hmm" Grandfather looks pensive

"And the war. That damn war. It took so much away; if it hadn't happened then things might have been better"

Grandfather points a finger at Tom without taking his hands of his walking stick "but it did happen. Things won't be any different, they are just the same. You can't change them"

"Yes...but...."

"Hey, you think that if the war hadn't have been you would have been any different? Would you have married Ellen if it wasn't for the war? You might have still been single. All conjecture"

Grandfather stabs the floor lightly with his walking stick

"What has been has happened, all that matters is now. Do you think moping will make things better? What you need is your family. Your child. She needs you. Think of little Ivy"

"Ivy?" asks Tom meekly

"Yes Ivy" Grandfather stabs the floor again "she needs you, and you have your whole life ahead of you. That's another thing you don't know, how long you've got. There's a tradition of long life in the Lane family... "

"But Father didn't live long"

"Don't you think I don't know that? He was my son. I'm grieving as well you know, life goes on"

Tom looks down

"You may live long but you never know. Live each day because when it's gone, it's gone. You can't say 'ooh, I'd like to try it again please but with this and that added, oh and take these bad things away'. No, you only get one life"

Tom looks up

"Look what you've achieved so far, who's to say what you will do next? You never stop Tom. You're always doing something. Everyone in the neighbourhood knows who you are. Family, friends, neighbours. They don't want to see a misery walking down the street, you inspire people. What they have seen is someone who went to war and came back"

"They don't care"

"About the war? Nooo. They just care about their own lives. But if they see someone who is cheery, it makes them feel better. Often they don't know why and can't attribute it to anything. I've seen the way you make people smile, especially when you play that piano"

"I don't have anything to be happy about"

"Of course you do. Ivy!"

Grandfather stabs the floor again with his stick "hmm?"

"I suppose"

"No suppose about it. You must continue to strive forward, whatever the problems. The feeling won't ever go away, I know that when I lost my wife. But I never gave up. If I was fit enough, I would have gone to the Front, eh?"

A smile starts to creep across Tom's face "you at the Front?"

"Why not? I would have given those Germans something to think about, not that I hate Germans mind"

Tom smirks at the thought of his Grandfather hobbling across No Mans Land on a walking stick with a Lee Enfield.

"That's the spirit" says Grandfather

The rest of the year Tom spends in mourning, however, he took on board his Grandfather's words and carries on the best he can, despite the illness. He throws himself into his music and plays whenever and wherever he can. The band still plays, not with the line up that got together after the war. With family life, band members come and go, but Tom is there still, playing his heart out. And when he can't play in the band, he'll play in whatever pub he is in at the time.

This particular evening sometime before Christmas Tom is in the Lancaster down in Kensington playing the piano. He is having a break and supping his beer. Ruby's father is there.

"Evening Mister Baker" says Tom

"Please, call me Bertram"

"Alright...Bertram"

"You play the piano well"

"Thank you; it's what I do best"

"How are coping without Ellen?"

"Well, I'm er... doing alright"

A cheer goes up on the other side of the pub. Bertram moves closer to Tom.

"Have you thought about our Ruby?" he says

"Ruby?"

"Yes, she would make a fine wife for you"

"Mister Baker!"

"Please, Bertram"

"No, I hadn't thought about it"

"Well do. She already looks after your daughter and you need someone to look after you too"

Before Tom can make any further thoughts on the subject, someone calls him back to the piano. He walks over then stops, turns and sees Bertram standing there with a smile on his face as he raises his beer glass towards Tom. He turns and carries on walking to the piano where he starts to play.

1924

Looking after Ivy is shared by Tom's mother and Mrs Bushnell. In the evenings, Ruby is still going round to Tom's to care for the child. She is getting ready to go round this evening after she had finished work.

"Off to Tom's" says her mother

"Yes" she says

"You're round there a lot, aren't you?" asks her father

"Ye-es"

"Have you thought about marrying him?" he asks in between puffs of his pipe

"Father?" she enquires

Mother pipes up "yes, how about it Ruby? We do need the space here; you can't carry on sleeping in the same room as your brothers. You're twenty, old enough to leave now"

"Are you trying to get rid of me?" Ruby wails

"He's a war hero, you know" says Bertram from behind a cloud of pipe smoke

"He has plenty of space at his home" says mother

"He has a car" Bertram said, leaning forward as if to reinforce the point.

"And the little girl knows you well. She needs a mother"

Ruby pulls her coat up over her shoulders and walks out without saying a further word.

Ruby had consoled Tom during his period of mourning. On this happy day, Ivy is a bridesmaid. Tom's new father-in-law is Bertram; he is a builder and decorator, there is something common between the two men as Tom's father had been a decorator. But now, Ruby is Tom's wife.

After photographs, the crowd gather round to 118 Malvern, in the corner of the living room is a record player, its huge horn sticks in the air playing the latest music. Ruby pulls Tom to the middle of the floor and starts to dance; he moves a little but quickly gets out of breath.

"It's called the Charleston" says Ruby

"I have to sit down love, sorry" gasps Tom

Ruby carried on dancing while the rest of the guests mill and chat. Ivy tries to dance but can't, although she doesn't care as she is having fun. Before Tom can sit down, Bertram accosts him

"Well lad, you'll not be disappointed with our Ruby"

"Thank you" he replies

Bertram walks off with a smile and Tom is just about to sit down when he sees his mother's face. She is as sour looking as ever and Tom knows that she disapproves of this marriage. Ruby is young compared to himself, and mother thinks of her as a floozy.

Tom sits down next to Uncle Albert.

"How are you feeling Tom?" asks Albert

"I'm faring alright" he replies "I can't manage this dancing lark though; I get right out of breath"

"No...this new fangled music. It's the new rage you know"

Tom thinks for a moment "it's alright, has a nice beat, foot tapper you know. It's the jazz I don't like"

Ruby dances while the two men continue to watch.

Albert says "you can see her calves you know"

"Sign of the times, old man"

"How far will it go? Soon they will be almost naked"

"Well, things are changing quickly now"

"She looks like a young boy with that haircut"

Tom turns his head quickly towards Albert

"She looks like my wife!"

Albert says "now she's married you, she can vote"

"No, that's married women over thirty; she's got another nine years yet"

"Whatever next, women voting"

"Oh come on, it's not that bad. Women helped greatly during the war, they deserve this"

The two men watch Ruby briefly before Tom asks his uncle "why didn't you go to war?"

"I was too old"

"So was father" Tom says "but he joined up"

"I know, damn fool"

"It wasn't the war that killed him though"

Albert replies "it's your mother I feel sorry for"

"Oh, I think she's coping. I go and see her a few times week. Besides, Liz and Ada are with her"

Albert then says "you're a war hero, you are Tom"

"I don't feel it" comes the reply

"Don't put yourself down"

"I'm not; I just feel that I lived while thousands of men died on the battlefield"

Brief silence.

"I hope there'll never be another war like that one" says Tom "I don't know how I got through the last one. I must have just have been lucky"

Drinks are being handed round; Tom and Albert grab a glass of wine each. Albert turns to Tom and says "well, the war's over now and I for one, wish you the best, Tom"

The two men chink their glasses, then turn to watch Ruby and Ivy dance.

After a brief honeymoon, Tom returns to work. He gasps for air constantly and wonders when his time is but apart from that things are going well and he continues working for the Post Office. He and Ruby move into 209 Portnall Road on the top floor, nice place, very similar to 96 Malvern.

The happy couple settle but before long, Albert is around again on August 30th.

"What's up, Albert?" enquires Tom

"It's you grandfather, he's asking for you"

Both men climb into the car and drive around to Chapter Road. Tom's other uncles are there. Tom walks through and stands by the bed where Grandfather William is lying who is wheezing.

"Tom" he says "come closer"

"Hello Grandfather"

"Tom, I just wanted to see you before I go"

"Go? Go where?"

"I've had a good life; I hoped my son would too"

Gran'pa William gives a cough

"I don't want you giving up on life, do you hear?"

"Huh?"

"You keep playing that piano, young Thomas"

Then he gasps his last breath and he is dead.

The room is quiet, Tom put his hand up to his breast, and he remembers the watch his father had given him. The same watch that he had inherited from his father, who is now lying here. The watch he has no more. Instead he has his grandfather's words and vows to himself he will do his best.

"I'll do my best, Grandfather"

Tom is at work and sees Frank.

"Hello Frank"

"Oh hello Tom" he replies "alright?"

"I'm fine" says Tom "but how's your mother?"

"Oh, she's not happy. She's still mourning her Ellen. She was her favourite you know"

"Is she going to come round, do you know?"

"I don't think she wants to see you, she still blames you for Ellen's death"

Tom says nothing while Frank lays an arm on his shoulder.

"She's a very stubborn woman; I can't get through to her"

"Thanks Frank"

"Well, I better be off on my round. See you later Tom"

Although Mrs Bushnell decides not to talk to Tom she still wants to see her grandchild. She comes round to visit Ruby when Tom is at work.

"Hello Mrs Bushnell"

Mrs Bushnell marches straight in.

"I want to see my grandchild"

"Well, she's right there"

"Hello Ivy" she says suddenly becoming very playful

"Gran'ma" the child runs towards Mrs Bushnell

Ellen senior turns to Ruby "I'm taking my grandchild to the park"

"But..." before she can say anything more

"She's not your child"

She takes Ivy by the hand

"And you are far too young for Thomas"

With that, Mrs Bushnell walks out with the child.

"Tom will be home soon" Ruby shouts

1926

Tom's band plays once a month, the Ralph Hussey Syncopators. He would like to play more but it is difficult to get band members to leave their families at home. The band line up changed yet again and it is getting more difficult to find decent musicians to fill the gaps. The band has just finished rehearsing.

"Alright chaps" says Tom "same time tomorrow?"

"No, I can't do it" says the trombone player "it's my daughter's birthday"

"The night after?"

"No, I can't do it. My wife has complained I'm out too much" says the double bass

"I'm available Wednesday next week" says the drummer

"Me too"

Everyone agrees that Wednesday next week would be fine; Tom closes the lid of the piano as the musicians pack their instruments.

"Haven't you had another child Tom?" asks the banjo player

"Yes" he replies "Dennis is his name"

"Don't you think you should stay at home more with your wife?"

"Oh, she's alright. She doesn't mind"

Everyone says their goodbyes and leave while Tom locks up the room and drops the keys into his pocket.

Tom starts his car up and gets in. He drives down the road and notices the radio shop so he stops to park up. He climbs out leaving the engine idling and stands facing the shop.

"I've never noticed this shop before" he says to himself

He takes a good look in through the window; he looks up at the sign above the window.

"Rex Radio"

"Radiograms for sale" reads the sign plastered to the inside of the window. Another reads "sale on phonograms"

"Huh!" says Tom to himself "all this new fangled technology"

He looks at the record player with its huge horn staring back at him, the grooves in the horn all lead the eye to the dark hole disappear at the back. He notices leaning up by the record player wooden body are some black discs; the sign reads "the latest music from New Orleans"

"That damn jazz" Tom mutters "what's wrong with music hall?"

Tom shuffles back to his car with his hands in his pockets. He turns round to have a final look through the window but in the reflection is a Tommy in full uniform standing behind him. He turns.

"Hello?"

No one is there.

"Any one there?" he looks up and down the road. There is no one in sight, the only noise he can hear is his car ticking over. He isn't sure, but the Tommy in the window looked like him. He shakes his head, climbs back into his car and drives off.

Tom is at work, sorting letters. Tea break, he goes to the small canteen and gets himself a tea. A co-worker sits next to him.

"How's the band?" he enquires

"Not good" replies Tom "it seems that not many people want to go out to see a band these days"

"Don't forget, people are losing their jobs you know"

"It doesn't cost much to go and see a band, why don't you come and see us?"

"Tom! Why should I go and see a band when I have the radiogram at home? I can listen to all that music in the comfort of me own home, and.....I can enjoy nice half while I'm listening. You can't do that in the venue"

"Hah, it's not the same. You can't get that live feel that you get with a band"

"It's good enough"

Tom sups the last of his tea and returns to work.

"Listen to the radio" he mutters to himself

1930

Frank turns up at Tom's.

"What's up Frank" he asks

"My mother, she wants to see Ivy"

"Why can't she come and see her for herself?"

"She ill. Very ill"

Ivy is made ready and the little troop drive down to Kensington. They walk into Mrs Bushnell's bedroom where she is lying. A doctor is listening to her heart with his stethoscope. Ivy walks over to the bed while Tom and Ruby stay at the door.

"Gran'ma, hello"

Mrs Bushnell turns her head

"Ivy, my little girl"

"We'll be downstairs" says Tom

Tom and Ruby sit downstairs in silence, with just the clock on the mantelpiece for company. Ivy comes downstairs.

"Gran'ma's very sick" she says

"I'm sure she'll be alright" says Ruby.

They wait for a while longer.

"Perhaps we should go" says Ruby

Frank comes downstairs.

"She's..." he tries to speak

Tom stands up and lays a hand on Frank's shoulder.

Frank croaks "I'm sorry she didn't see eye to eye with you"

"Frank" starts Tom "It's quite alright. She was a good person. I think she was angry at losing her daughter and saw me as the one to blame"

Frank nods his head

"I have no grudges against her. I've seen too many bad things to have bad feelings"

1933

Tom has been working at the Post Office for years now but is taking many days off ill. Even with the car, he is unable to get into work some days and he has coughing fits that last for hours. At the end of his shift Tom is called into the Postmaster's office.

"Sit down Tom"

He sits down and waited while Mister Walters put his papers away.

"It seems you have been taking quite a few days off sick"

Tom sat in silence.

"I know about your injury you sustained during the war that made you sick..."

Tom still sits there.

"But that was sixteen years ago now. It's clear to me that this injury is a permanent one and that you will never get better. That is why I'm going to ask you to take early retirement"

"But I don't want to retire" protests Tom "I like my job. Besides, don't you know there's mass unemployment at the moment?"

"I do read the newspapers you know. Besides, it's mainly up north where they have the most problems"

"Even so, I want to keep my job. I'm forty three and I'll probably won't get another job"

"It's alright Tom. It's just a recommendation. But you do need to come to work otherwise I will make an official request to retire you"

"Right" says Tom "I'll try my best" Tom doesn't want to retire from a well paid job. Not only does he have to pay for his daughter but he also has a seven year old son.

"Alright, that is all"

Tom leaves the office, and work. He has been saving his thirty three shillings a week wages for a few years and now he has something to do.

Ivy came home from school, along with her younger brother Dennis.

"Hello Peggy" says Ruby. No one calls her Ivy anymore apart from officials, everyone knows her as Peggy now.

"Hello Mother. Where's Father?"

Ruby stops what she is doing and thinks for a moment,

"I don't know, he should be home by now. He probably went straight down the pub"

Tom sticks his head round the door "come on" he says then disappears.

Ruby, Peggy and Dennis rush downstairs "what was Tom up to this time?" thinks Ruby. They step outside and he is sitting in a large car. It is a Ford V8; he has traded in his old Model T and bought himself an even bigger car.

"Come on, get in" he says

They all climb in as the engine roars into life; Tom put the car into gear and pulls away down Portnall Road. It isn't long before they reach the countryside along the main Harrow Road. The car races along the road through the village of Stonebridge and then Wembley sometimes at speeds of fifty or sixty miles per hour. There are no speed limits and soon they are approaching South Harrow. Off in the distance they can see the spires of Harrow school but the car isn't going there and turns off down Rayners Lane, a small country road.

"Where are we going Dad?" asks Peggy

"I don't know, I'm just driving. We'll see, eh?"

They stop at a pub called The Rayners in the middle of a village where there aren't many shops but there is nearby a train station. They settle down for a meal and a drink, soft pop for Peggy and Dennis though as they are under age but they don't care as they are enjoying themselves immensely. Tom can hear the birds singing, which always lifts his heart.

"This is lovely" says Ruby

"Yes, I used to come here often" says Tom

"When did you ever come here?" she enquires

"When I used to do shooting practice during the war. There was a shooting range down the road there" he points southwards.

Ruby thought it strange as Tom rarely mentioned the war before now.

"So, you did know where you were going" she smiles

"How about we drive down to Dorset next week? How does that sound?"

Both Ruby and the children are overjoyed and agree that it is a great idea. Sitting in the sunshine in the countryside outside the pub is far away from the drudgery of the war even if it was sixteen years ago, Tom still thinks about those days. Now he is relaxed and reasonably well, hopefully trying to put behind him the horrors he witnessed all those years ago.

CHAPTER 13

CHANGES FOR EVERYONE

1936

THINGS HAVE BEEN GOING WELL for Tom; he kept his job up until now. The Government introduced driving tests which he had to take but he passed, and now has a full driving licence. Speed limits of 30 miles per hour have been introduced in urban areas, which meant he has to slow his driving down. Peggy had moved out of the house and relocated to Bristol and Ruby is expecting another child. Although the term 'well' is used loosely for Tom, 'well' is being alive. He still coughs, hacks, wheezes and has trouble walking; not that he bothers walking anymore but drives everywhere. But he is still quite ill with his coughing fits and any exertion produces wheezing, sometimes he gets so bad that he can't even make it out of the door and spends the day gasping for air in his armchair.

Ruby suggests that they go down to Dorset again for the summer as it might help with Tom's bad lungs. They all climb into the big car and Tom starts up, he drives down through Kensington to join the Kensington High Street that takes the party to Chiswick and beyond into the countryside. They drive for two hours and stop at Stonehenge where they marvel at the stones, walking in between the large monoliths. They have done this a few times before but still the wonder of this place hasn't diminished with each visit. After a quick picnic between the stones, they pack up and drive on down to Dorset. They arrive at their destination at Swanage, book into the Greyhound Hotel in Corfe.

Ruby wants to walk but can't because of the child she is carrying, this suit Tom fine as he can't walk very far either. They spend their days sitting on the beach and let Dennis make sandcastles. Tom listens to the waves breaking on the sand and it calms him, the fresh air helping with his breathing, but he is bored and wants to go home.

"Not this time" he thinks to himself.

They are there a week, have a lovely holiday and return home, Tom feeling better for it.

In October, Ruby has her child, a girl they name Brenda, and however, Tom's condition worsens. Pollution in the city had increased over the years with heavier traffic, car sales had rocketed when the depression ended, as well as the introduction of combustion engined buses and taxis. There are factories nearby, especially the new car factory in Kensal Rise. The roads are clogged with vehicles and the exhaust fumes don't help with Tom's breathing although he likes living in London and has no intention of moving out. He has lived here all his life and everyone knows him, but it doesn't help and he spends days hacking and coughing in his armchair when he should be at work.

He has many days like this off sick from work, he is not a well man and coughs for hours on end and often try and catch his breath with the least effort, his fellow postal workers show concern but Tom just says it was nothing. He had lost his father, his wife and the war has a lasting effect on him mentally. Eventually, sometime in November, the Postmaster had to do something and calls Tom into his office.

"Tom" he says "you have been taking a lot of days off lately, you must be very ill".

He replies "no I'm fine Mister Walters. There's little wrong with me, a little cough now and then; but who doesn't get a cold this time of year?"

"I'm sorry Tom but I have to send you to the company doctor"

Tom protests "I'm well!"

"Sorry, but you were asked to retire three years ago and you should have taken it"

He reluctantly agrees to the appointment.

Tom turns up at the doctors' office, knocks and waits for the "come in".

He walks in, Doctor Murray is writing his notes "please sit down" he says, "I understand you have had a lot of time off"

"Just a cold here and there, nothing serious"

"Let me be the judge of that, strip off down to your underwear"

He goes behind the screen and takes off his clothes down to his underwear and socks. The doctor listens to his patient's breathing with his stethoscope, measures his pulse and looks down his throat.

"Say aaah"

"Aaaaah"

After a while and few more tests the doctor is sure what he saw and what he read in his patient's notes that this man has serious breathing problems. The doctor looks pensive; eventually he speaks "you served in the war, didn't you?"

"Yes, at Passchendaele"

"Hmm, and you were gassed"

"Oh yes, just a little bit of gas. I was alright after though"

"I'm afraid you are very ill, your lungs have been seriously and permanently damaged. I will recommend that you be put forward for pension".

"Oh come on, I'm not that ill" says Tom with a cough "I've got lots of life left in me"

"I'm sorry but I give you....." a pause "....six months at the most"

"Not likely, I bet you ten bob I'll outlive you"

"Done" says the doctor losing his seriousness for a brief moment before recovering his composure "but I will still write my report"

Tom goes home reeling from the news but feeling confident that he will live longer than the doctor had predicted, after all, he'd lived this long. He would have to tell Ruby sooner or later, and with another child just born, how will he feed his family on a pension? On the way home he stops of at his mother's house.

"Hello mother" he says in a cheery voice

"Don't hello me in that happy tone" she replies "I suppose you want a cup of tea"

"That would be lovely"

Adeline put the kettle on the hob and lights the gas, she is an old lady now and as grumpy as ever. But she is fit as a fiddle and moves around lithely for a sixty eight year old. Tom compares himself with her. He is the old one; he can hardly walk any distance.

"I don't suppose you could dig a small patch of garden for me, could you?" she asks

Tom is taken aback a little then thinks "why not?"

"It's my back, it's killing me" she says

He goes out in the back garden and starts to dig, not frantically but calmly and slow. He had lots of experience with a spade but doesn't want to go as far as digging a trench. He finds he can do this all day as there are frequent breaks in between turning over the soil; he doesn't get out of breath with this and thinks "now here is something I could do". It is something at last to give himself some exercise and this inspires him to think about finding another job. Tom sits down and has some home made pea soup his mother made for him. He slurps a spoonful.

"Ooh, I love your pea soup" he says

He goes through a few more spoonfuls.

"I've been pensioned off from my job" he finally says

"Oh, you'll be able to have more time to do my garden" she says without sympathy.

Tom silently chuckles to himself, but quickly pulls himself together as he still has to tell Ruby.

It is a week since Tom first dug his Mother's garden.

"Hello my love" he cheerily says to Ruby

She stands with a stern face with her arms crossed.

"Why didn't you tell me?" she asks

"Tell you what?" he replies

"You know full well" she wags a finger at Tom's face "I heard"

"Heard what?"

"You lost your job. A good job too"

"Who told you?"

"It doesn't matter who, I know"

"Well, I'm ill" says Tom

"I know you are, but you should have told me instead of me hearing through gossip. You seem to forget sometimes that everybody around here knows you"

There are times, he thinks, he wishes he isn't so well known.

"Sorry, I just wanted to wait until the right time to tell you"

"You'll have to find another job; your pension won't keep us all, especially now Brenda is here"

Tom sits down in his armchair.

"What can I do? The least little effort sends me into a wheezing fit"

"There's a grocers down in Canterbury that's looking for someone"

"A grocer?"

"Yes, he'll be willing to take you on. I'm sure he's an ex-soldier"

"I don't know..."

"At least try it. Go now and speak to him. He knows me, I'm sure he'll give you the job. It's better than nothing"

Tom stands up and put his jacket on.

"Alright, just this once"

He drives round to Canterbury Road. He sees the pub there; it makes him stop and think for a moment before he quickly regains his senses and sees the grocer at number 96. French's is the name so he parks up and walks in.

"Can I speak to Mister French please?" he asks

"Yes, that's me. Frederick French, proprietor. Are you Tom Lane?"

"Yes, that's me"

Mr French takes Tom's hand and shakes it.

"You're a war hero you know. I got injured myself too, shrapnel. At the Somme"

"Indeed" says Tom

"You must be looking for the job as my assistant"

Tom starts to speak.

"Your wife was here yesterday, she said you lost your job at the Post Office"

"Was she now?"

"All I need you to do is to move vegetables around and sometimes serve customers, can you do that?"

"Yes" replies Tom "I can do that"

"Good, when can you start?"

"Is now a good time?"

Mr French laughs, joined in by Tom. He goes to the back of the shop and brings back an overcoat.

"You can start by bringing the carrots in from the back"

Tom smiles and put his coat on.

He likes this job and talks happily to the customers, although the job doesn't pay much it does top up his pension. His health seems to improve too as there is little effort involved in the job, except when he has to carry in a heavy bag of vegetables. But that is alright as he can sit down afterwards and catch his breath. And a bonus too,

Mister French has a radio in the shop and on occasions, turns it on. Tom especially likes the Music Hall but, and this is something he shares with Mister French, he doesn't like the jazz.

"Jazz?" he says "not my cup of tea"

"Too many notes" replies Tom

1938

He still has his job and a small pension, plus tips from playing the piano in the pub. But it isn't as much as his postal wages were. He is struggling.

"Tom" says Ruby "I need some money. Dennis needs new shoes"

"I don't have any; you've already taken what I've earned"

"Then you'll have to stop going down the pub"

"What?" he sits bolt upright "I like my drink down at the local"

"Well, we need more money"

He sits thinking for a while

"And the rent's due tomorrow" she says

He thinks some more "what can we cut out?"

"Perhaps we can sell the car" says Ruby

Tom is really put out now but his wife does have a point. The car isn't really necessary any more as he doesn't have to walk miles, just to the grocer store, and he thinks, the pub. But his big black shiny car. He loves that car. But he loves his beer more. And he loves playing the piano down the pub even more.

"Alright, I'll sell the car" he says

"Are you sure?" she asks

"We need the money" he says, then he thinks to himself "and the beer"

Ruby looks at her husband sympathetically.

"Straight after work tomorrow, I'll drive round to the second hand car sales"

Ruby sits on the arm of Tom's chair and put her arm round his shoulders.

"Shame really, I do enjoy our visits down to Dorset"

The car sold, Tom sits in his armchair reading his newspaper. He is a worried man.

"What's the matter Tom?" asks Ruby noticing the worry in Tom's face

"It's the events happening in Europe"

"Why should that worry us?"

"Well, the last something like this happened, we went to war"

"Yes, but they wouldn't go to war again, surely?"

"I remember saying that meself back then. Even when people told me I still told them 'no, we won't ever go to war' but I was wrong"

He lifts up the newspaper again.

"It says here that the government are handing out gas masks to everyone"

He lowers the paper.

"They must be worried themselves to do something like that"

"Well, you had better collect ours then"

"Tomorrow...I'll do it tomorrow during my lunch break"

A neighbour from downstairs appears and says that there is someone to see Mister Lane. Tom walks downstairs and is confronted by a man wearing a suit with a clipboard.

"Are you Thomas Lane?" he asks

"Yes I am" replies Tom

"Oh"

"Anything wrong?"

"Well, we thought somebody else was claiming your pension as we thought you would be dead, The doctor's notes say that you only had six months left in...let me see now...ahh two years ago"

"Ohno, I'm very much alive"

"Oh, are you sure?"

"Of course I am. I may not be fit as a fiddle but I'm well and truly here. Tell me, is Doctor Murray still alive?"

"No, he died last year"

Tom makes fist "ha, I knew it. I outlived him. I don't suppose I'll get my ten bob though"

The man looks quizzically at Tom.

"Sorry, it was a bet we made with each other. I'm sorry to hear he has passed away"

The man now satisfied then leaves while Tom closes the door and thinks about going to the pub to spend his hard earned ten shillings that he doesn't have.

Tom comes home a bit later than usual, and out of breath.

"Tom? Are you alright?" asks Ruby

"Oh yes" he says and dumps a large bag on the kitchen table

"What's that?" she comes over and peers into the bag.

"I got them" he says as he pulls out a gas mask.

Dennis, sitting at the table reaches out and his father hands the gas mask to him.

"We are going to have a practice" demands Tom

He slips a mask over his head and the container falls by his waist, Dennis does the same with a little clumsiness. Smiling, Ruby slips hers on then she looks at Tom then turns to Dennis. Both fall into fits of laughter. Tom looks through the holes stands motionless, watching his wife and son in hysterical laughter. He slips back into 1917 and he is in the trenches and wearing a gas mask. A yellow-green tinged gas is floating all around him. He is panting and the heat of the mask inside is overwhelming.

Suddenly another gas masked figure appears, it is Sergeant Knight. He marches quickly up along the trench and up close to Tom's masked face.

"Don't you take that mask off, my son" he mumbles through his gas mask "you'll die"

More soldiers appear all wearing masks too. They dance around Tom "you'll die, you'll die"

A shell lands at his feet and opens, releasing its deadly gas in a swirling green mist, he looks down with eyes wide open. His breathing gets heavier and heavier while the soldiers still dance and the sergeant shouts "don't take it off!"

The soldiers continue their dance "you'll die' you'll die"

Tom can't stand anymore and whips off the gas mask, he stands there in the trench holding his mask in hand by his hip and the soldiers still dance.

"NOOOOOOO!"

He stands there in the kitchen, sweat dripping down his forehead. Ruby takes off her mask, then Dennis.

"Are you alright, Love?" she asks. She walks up to him, Dennis sits still.

"Ye-es. I'm fine" Tom stammers

"Is it the war?" she asks

"Yes" he replies

"The gas?"

"Yes"

She holds up a gas mask and looks at it

"Sorry Ruby, gas is a serious business"

Tom lays a hand on Dennis' shoulder.

"I'm alright now"

It is nearing the end of 1938, and the New Year brings much the same. Tom still has his grocery job but has to walk everywhere now which doesn't help his breathing much, but he copes. After work, he still goes down the pub to play his beloved piano and people love it.

All is well with Tom, until....

CHAPTER 14

HERE WE GO AGAIN

1939

SEPTEMBER AND TOM IS STILL working as a greengrocer. His health hasn't got worse at all and he feels quite fit although he still gets out of breath because he doesn't make demands on his body, he has readjusted his life to cope with the illness. He still goes round his mothers' to dig her garden. Although she is still a misery, she is happy in her own way pottering round her garden. Upstairs lives Ada and her husband Charlie, and also Liz and her husband Bertie. Adeline is pleased to see Tom every so often, although she never shows it.

Tom however is concerned at events happening in Europe where the Germans have marched into Austria and Czechoslovakia. "It was Austria last time wasn't it?" Tom reminds himself "it was that country that started the Great War." He is concerned, he'd seen it before and thought, and hoped it wouldn't happen again.

September the third and Tom walks to work as usual, he pops into the newsagent to buy his regular journal. On this fine morning he walks into the shop when he sees the headlines.

"GERMANY INVADES POLAND"

"No!" he stops in his tracks "they can't be doing it again?"

He quickly buys the newspaper and carries on walking to work.

"What's up Tom? Looks like you've seen a ghost" enquires Mister French.

"This!" Tom said holding up the newspaper "those Germans are at it again. I thought they learnt their lesson from the last time"

The shop owner studies the newspaper while Tom throws his hat down "don't these people ever learn. I suppose war will be declared again"

"Get that radio on" the shop owner says.

An hour passes and a lady comes into the shop as Tom sits down on a sack of potatoes just to get his breathe.

"I'd like some potatoes" she asks

Tom immediately stands up even though the potato bin is full and there is no need to go into the sack.

"And a cabbage please"

He sits down on the sack of potatoes again. He suddenly turns his head towards the radio; he hears the presenter's voice, he walks over and turns the radio up.

"...this is the home service; we are going over to Downing Street to hear an announcement by the Prime Minister....."

"Ssh! It's Chamberlain" says Tom "he's going to speak"

"I am speaking to you from the Cabinet Room at 10 Downing Street"

Mr French and the customer move closer to the radio.

"This morning the British Ambassador in Berlin handed the German Government a final note stating that unless we heard from them by 11 o'clock that they were prepared at once to withdraw their troops from Poland, a state of war would exist between us. I have to tell you now..."

A young man joins the small crowd listening to the radio.

"...that no such undertaking has been received, and consequently this country is at war with Germany"

The young man turns and walks out of the shop, he says to his friend waiting outside "we're at war with Germany"

Tom's shoulders drop, he is in deep despair. Although he is too old and wouldn't be fit enough to join the army, the technology has come a long way. The firepower in the Great War totally destroyed the landscape in Belgium. What would the new weaponry do now?

"Oh those Germans" the customer says "never mind, our boys will sort them out. Well we did last time"

She walks out with her vegetables. Tom said rather glumly "she doesn't look old enough to remember the last war. She wasn't even there. I was and we didn't finish the war by Christmas like they said. It was total devastation. How long will this war last?"

Mister French lays a hand on Tom's shoulder.

"I understand" he says

Tom's rehearsal with the band is tonight, they congregate in their room they normally use for their practice; Tom gets his papers together and starts to speak "tonight chaps, I think we should do...."

The drummer cuts in quickly "before we start, I'd like to point out that it may not be worth carrying on with the band"

Tom is stunned; it was several seconds before he can speak "what...why?"

"Well" says the drummer "I've signed up for the army. I start training next week"

Tom's hands holding his papers drop into his lap.

The double bass also tells Tom he had joined up.

"We might as well go home"

Everyone slowly departs, leaving Tom on his own with his papers. Tom sits thinking about getting some younger people in "oh, those young people won't want to join a music hall band. They like all that stuff coming from America"

Tom decides to go down the pub to console himself.

"Hello Tom" is the greeting he got from Lionel as he walks through the entrance.

He greets back, he is down but not rude. He is heeding his grandfather's words and tries to be as happy as he can.

"It seems..." he starts "...that the band has disbanded"

"Yes, but you can still play the piano though, can't you?"

"Oh yes, I won't give that up"

Ralph leans over and says "have you thought about being a warden, Tom?"

"No"

"Eh! Enough of that don't change the subject. Tom, on that piano, there's half a beer in it for you"

The alcohol is little incentive, just a bonus. As usual, he doesn't need much encouragement and makes his way to the piano. Ralph who suggested the warden just stands there with his mouth open and his finger raised. There is no point carrying on, he sups his beer and moves his way to the crowd that is now gathering round the piano. Tom sits down, but he has a slight nagging thought "a warden". Then he stops thinking and starts playing.

The next day, Tom is at work.

"Someone mentioned about being a warden last night" he says to his boss

"Oh, I think that would suit you. Have you thought about joining up?"

"Maybe...maybe"

Lunchtime and Tom walks to the Police station. In he goes and half an hour later, he comes out with his black helmet with a white W painted on the front.

1940

Tom and Ruby has another child in April named Frances but it is not a good time for a child to be born in the middle of a war. Just like before, the Germans brought the battle to the citizens of Britain only this time, their technology was far superior. Bigger planes that could carry far bigger payloads and the newspapers had pictures of buildings in London that were alight. Again, just like last time, many men between eighteen and forty were gone, sent to Europe to fight.

Tom is down the pub playing the piano like he does most nights; he must have played in every pub in West London by now. This time is different, he still plays his heart out just as usual, but a heavy weight is on his shoulders. He has seen towns and villages razed to the ground, men blown up and other men with such horrendous injuries. This Hitler chap, he seems far worse than the Kaiser was and he is taking his people back to war again. Tom refuses to believe that the German people themselves are bad; it was just the nutters at the top. Still, he keeps Grandfathers words with him and tries to keep his pecker up as it were, and be cheerful, however difficult.

Closing time and he walks home in the darkness, there are no street lights on. He looks up to the sky, the stars shine brilliantly, something he hasn't seen since before the first war. He is fascinated by the brightness they shine with; he can recognise many of the constellations. Carrying on, he can see a slit of light from someone's window where the owner hasn't quite closed their blackout curtains properly. He cups his hands over his mouth.

"Close your curtains! There's a light showing"

The slit of light disappears. He carries on and makes it home.

He creeps in knowing the children would be in bed, he finds Ruby asleep too and quietly slips into bed. He drifts off but his mind couldn't keep off the war and he drifts back to Flanders. He can't sleep and turns over onto his back and lay there staring at the dark ceiling. The black curtains are up creating a near total darkness. Suddenly sirens go off.

"Air raid" Tom says. They had many of these but the planes never come over here, he thinks that he had better be safe and get everyone downstairs.

"Air raid" he says again as he picks up his torch and helmet.

"What?" murmurs Ruby as she slowly came round.

"Come on, get the children up"

She can hear the sirens wailing now, everyone in the flat clambers out of bed and rush down the stairs. The family manages to fit into the tight space that is under the stairs on the bottom floor. They can hear the drone of the planes in the darkness, they can hear the explosions of the bombs and they sound very close. Tom freezes and he starts to remember the trench days, he is back with his unit as they duck for cover in the pillbox. He turns to see his comrades running towards the safety of the concrete bunker but they never make it. The man behind is blown to bits while the leading man falls down to the ground, his body peppered with shrapnel. Then there is a loud crash as a bomb explodes on the floors above them that brings Tom back, debris comes flying down and causes the stairway to partially collapse. Suddenly there is the tinkle of piano keys as the whole instrument crashes within a meter of where everyone is. It is his own piano. Finally, there is just the noise of bits of small bits of masonry falling over rubble; eventually it is quiet apart from plane engines in the distance.

"Is everyone alright?" he says, and one by one he gets a reply, he knows baby Frances is alive because she is crying. He pushes away the debris, bits of wood and a few bricks, it is only twenty minutes and the sirens start off again to give the all clear but it seems like hours. Tom looks up and can see the stars; there are gaping holes in the roof and floors of this building.

They trudge round to Tom's mother with what little they could salvage, and she put them up. After a restless nights sleep, he gets up and walks round to the house. The top has caved in and only the bottom floor survives, filled with bricks and wood. He returns back and they all sit in the kitchen while his mother makes tea.

"Don't you think it would be a good idea to send the girls away?" he asks Ruby

"What, evacuate them?" she looks up from feeding Frances

"Yes, they'll be safer"

"They'll be safer with us, here"

Tom stops talking; he knows it's useless to argue with Ruby.

In the afternoon after work, he goes round to his mothers only to be told that Ruby had found somewhere else, next door. He walks straight to 211 Portnall Road, somehow that flat has remained intact while builders are clearing rubble from 209. Ruby sticks her head out the window "Tom, up here!"

"Marvellous" he thinks "top floor again"

Ruby doesn't like being on the ground floor, she feels unsafe. Tom slowly climbs the stairs and walks into the front room.

"Hello Tom" says Ruby "I remembered this flat being empty for quite a while. I was pleased when I asked and told it was available"

The room has little furniture and looks bare. Frances is asleep while Brenda plays in the corner, Dennis is sitting cross legged on the floor with a hankie spread out flat. On the hankie are small pieces of metal.

"What are those?" asks Tom

"Pieces of shrapnel" Dennis replies

"Where did you get those from?"

"Next door. I found them in the rubble"

"Hmm! I don't think you should be rummaging around in bomb sites"

"It's alright, the workmen made sure I was safe. These will be the envy of the other boys at school"

Tom smiles then turns to look at the near wall.

"I'll have to see about a piano for there" he says

"Well, I think furniture would be a better idea"

Saturday morning at work, Tom realises he has left his sandwiches at home.

"There's not enough time to go home and get my lunch. I'll have to get something from the cafe"

"Alright Tom" says Mister French

Tom has just put his jacket on and is straightening up his collar at the back, when Dennis comes into the shop.

"You forgot this Dad" he says

"Oh, thanks Dennis"

He takes his coat off again.

"Is that your son?" asks Mister French

"Yes, this is Dennis"

"All these years you've worked here, that's the first time I've seen him"

Mister French takes a bunch of bananas of a shelf and hands them to Dennis

"Take this home for your mother" he says

"Thanks Fred" says Tom

Before anything else is said, a loud droning noise is heard along with the sirens and all three go outside into the street and look up. In the distance are hundreds of German bomber planes flying in formations.

"Wow" says Dennis "look at that Dad"

Explosions are heard in the distance.

"I think we had better get to the shelters"

"No, they're too far away" says Dennis

"Nonetheless, I think we should get to the shelters"

An explosion goes off a mile or so in the distance, but the shock wave can be felt. Tom briefly stands still, the memory of the explosions still haunt him from all those years ago. The planes continue flying as the anti-aircraft guns can be heard. Puffs of smoke can be seen amongst the planes as the anti-aircraft shells go off, but none of the bombers are hit. Tom gets agitated, but Dennis just stands his ground in fascination.

Suddenly a loud whizz, and above them are two spitfires hurtle past, they can't be more than 200 metres high and they made a noise so loud that Tom closes his eyes in terror. Dennis however jumps up and down with joy.

"Spitfires Dad, look at them" the young lad says

The two planes speed upward towards the bombers when from nowhere come two German fighter planes. The small planes engage each other in a dogfight while the bombers continue dropping their bombs over in the east somewhere, Tom thinks it might have been the docks on the Thames. Dennis continues to watch as one of the Messerschmitt planes speeds off in the opposite direction with smoke trailing behind it.

"We've got one Dad" says an excited Dennis

"I really think we should get inside son"

The bombers start to bank off with the beginning of their return run, by this time more Spitfires had reached the sky. One by one, a plane descends in flames, both enemy and Allied. This continues for ten minutes as the remaining bombers fly away, and what's left of the British Air Force return to their respective bases.

The sirens sound the all clear as Tom breathes a sigh of relief.

"Come on Dennis, you had better go home"

"Alright Dad. I'll see you later"

Tom turns to go back inside.

"He's a fine lad" says Mister French

"If a little boisterous" replies Tom

"To be expected from young boys, though"

"Indeed. I think I was a bit like that myself before I went to the Front"

CHAPTER 15

WE WON AGAIN...FOR WHAT?

Later, Tom lay in bed thinking about the planes, so many of them and so big. He turns to look at Ruby who is asleep, she looks so peaceful, so beautiful lying there. The light of the moon beamed through the window lighting up her face. He starts to drift off himself and finally falls asleep.

He was dreaming about the planes he saw, hundreds of them. They just seem to multiply until the sky is filled with planes that blot out the sun. Slowly, the Heinkels morph into Gothas. Thousands of them are filling the sky. He turns to see Dennis standing next to Mister French, but they are outside the Carlton pub.

"Run to the trenches" he shouts as he runs across the road and jumps into a trench. There are so many planes that it became dark now but he could still see his son standing at the entrance of the pub. A flare goes up and he pushes himself flat against the corrugated iron wall, as he had done on many occasions but he notices he was now wearing his army uniform. An explosion goes off, the dirt flies over Tom, the pieces of mud and stones rain down on him. He slides down the wall to a sitting position where he clutches his gun. The mud squelches as his backside reaches the floor. He sits rocking back and forth.

"No, I want to go home" he wails

Another explosion and he waits for the dirt to come over, but none come. Instead, a bunch of bananas fall on the trench floor.

"Oh no!" he wails

Another explosion, Tom waits for the debris to fall on him but a boot falls into the mud. Tom looks at it, he sits back as he realises that the owner's foot is still in it. Then a hand falls right next to him, he recoils in horror. He calms down a bit when a head falls on his lap. It's Big Bob, then the eyes open.

"Why didn't you get here earlier Tom?" says Bob's head

Tom pushes it off his lap where it comes to a rest on the mud, still looking at him.

"If you had come earlier Tom, I wouldn't have been killed"

"No, I came when I was ordered, I had no choice"

"Many men died because you weren't there Tom, men who could have been saved"

"I would have made no difference Bob"

"All those men, in the trenches while you were at home enjoying yourself"

"I'm just doing my job. GO AWAY!"

He sits up quickly, sweat pouring down his forehead.

"I'm just doing my job" he whispers

"What?" murmurs Ruby

"It's alright Love, just a bad dream Go back to sleep"

He gets up and walks into the children's bedroom. He checks Dennis is asleep, then over to check Brenda is safe in her bed. He desperately wants to send both girls away, to safety. They shouldn't be here, London is bombed almost everyday in some weeks. She had wriggled during the night so that the blanket had moved down, leaving her exposed to the cold. He reaches over and pulls the blanket up over Brenda.

He walks back to his own bedroom and quickly checks on Frances. She is awake, waving her arms around; she doesn't make a sound but just stares into open air. She notices her father creeping up on her and smiles a toothless grin. Tom picks her up and walks to the window, there are no lights anywhere but an eerie orange glow in the sky.

"That's London on fire" he whispers to the baby.

Frances gurgles.

"Those people. Those poor people"

He quietly slips Frances back into her cot, then slides himself back into bed. He lays staring at the ceiling for quite a while before falling asleep.

Tom is playing the pub when the sirens go off; he stops playing straight away and gets his helmet out and puts it on his head. Everyone stops what they are doing and listen to the bombs going off around them.

"Turn the lights out!" he says sternly to the landlord.

All the lights go out and Tom turns his torch on. Suddenly the pub shakes and bits of plaster come down. He goes round checking the curtains and tries to reassure people. After twenty minutes the planes have gone and the sirens give the all clear. He goes outside and looks around the street, the houses across the road are demolished.

He picks up a bucket of sand and walks over. Some people are running around in a panic.

"There's a bomb, it's going off" they shout

Someone had a bucket of water poised and ready to be thrown over the fire.

"Stop!" shouts Tom "that's an incendiary device. You'll make it worse"

He guides the man away, walks over to the device that flashed with a white flame. He pours the sand out of the bucket over the small bomb.

"Will it go off?" asks the man

The sand covered the burning bomb and the flame died down.

"No" replies Tom "it just burns with a white flame. It's to give the bombers something to aim for"

He put the bucket down and starts to push bits of wood away. The fire brigade have turned up; with the help of locals many bodies had been found. Tom sits on a pile of bricks in despair while more firemen and ambulance men arrive and are milling around, he is in deep despair and puts his head in his hands.

"Tom"

He looks up and there is his Grandfather standing on a pile of bricks with his walking stick.

"What are doing?" he asks Tom

"What?"

"Did you not listen to my words? You're sitting there moping again. So what if someone's died?"

"But..."

"No buts, the dead can't worry. Forget them; it's the living you need to help. Pull yourself together"

He lifts up and points his walking stick towards Tom.

"Yes Grandfather"

One of Tom's friends comes up to him.

"Who are you talking to Tom?" he says "are you alright?"

"I'm fine" Tom stands up "we need to get these bodies out"

The two men shift brick after brick and pull a dead woman clear and lay her on the ground.

"Ssh" says Tom

Both men stand and listen.

"There!" he points to the area they had just removed the woman from; they can hear a child's voice. They both simultaneously grab bricks and a child's hand appears from under a wooden beam, they keep digging until they expose a little girl crying. They pull her out and immediately she throws her hands around Tom's neck.

"It's alright love" he says "you're alright now"

"I want my Mummy" she wails

"Sorry love" says Tom "but your....Mummy's gone to heaven"

"That's not my Mummy" she cries

Tom stops in his tracks, he hands the girl to the other man "here, look after her"

He frantically starts digging again, throwing bricks out behind him. He suddenly comes across a hand, then an arm. Soon a face appeared, and the woman splutters.

"Alright missus, you'll be alright" as he carries on moving bricks, by now some fireman had come to Tom's aid.

"Where's my little girl?" says the woman.

"Don't worry, she's safe" replies a fireman

Eventually the woman is hauled out and is re-united with her daughter. They sit in an ambulance together, the doors close and they are on their way to the hospital.

The bodies of several people lay covered up on the ground, lights have been set up as police, firemen and ambulance men are frantically working to bring order back to the area. A police officer comes over to Tom.

"Thank you for your help Mister Lane. We can carry on from here, go home now"

"Thank you officer" he says and he turns to walk home.

1944

Tom and Ruby are out with Dennis and the girls; they all have their gas masks in their respective shoulder bags. "They're a nuisance" Ruby thinks to herself, "but necessary".

"I want ice lolly" shouts Frances

"Yes" agrees Brenda "ice lolly"

Tom put his hand in his pocket; there is a sound of coins.

"I'll see what there is"

He walks into a shop leaving Brenda and Frances standing by a sign that reads "ices", which has a line drawn through it, underneath is written "carrot 1d".

Out comes Tom holding two carrots, each impaled on a stick.

"There you go" he says as he hands each one to the girls.

"But that's not an ice lolly" says Brenda

"I want ice lolly" wails Frances

"I'm sorry, that's all there is. There are no ice lollies" says their father.

Tom and Ruby look at each other. How do you explain rationing to children?

Before either could come up with an explanation, there is a buzzing sound in the sky, it is a doodlebug and it sounds close. Then the silence. They all start to run for the nearest shelter, but even young Frances can run faster than Tom. They all manage to reach the safety of a heavy stone building but Tom is gasping for breath, and has difficulty keeping up with them.

"Come on Tom" shouts Ruby

"Come on Dad" shouts Dennis

He is really gasping now and he is just two metres from the corner of the building, the doodlebug hit then the massive explosion. Just as Tom makes it, debris flies everywhere. Clang, makes the sound of bits of metal. Tac tac tac make the sounds of small pieces of brick and stone. He is really wheezing now.

"You children alright?" asks Ruby, to which they reply they are.

"Tom?" she asks, but there is no reply as he is back at Passchendaele. The same scene replays again, he is running, just as he done many times. This time though, he can't move. His legs are moving but he stays on the same spot, the more he runs, the more frantic he becomes. The other soldiers are calling out from the bunker.

"Tom" they shout "run Tom"

He turns to look behind him, his comrades Archie and Ed are the same; they are running but stay on the same spot. Then the whistling noise and the two men are blown to pieces.

"Tom" shout the soldiers

He turns forward, his comrades are frantically calling him on, but he can't move.

"Tom" comes Ruby's voice

The last "Tom" brings him back to reality.

Ruby asks if he is all right

"I'm fine" he says

"Perhaps we should send the children away" she says

Tom and Ruby have finally made a decision to move the children out of London. Bristol is a good idea as Peggy has a house there although Dennis decides to stay, he is eighteen and works, Brenda and Frances have their suitcases packed and their coats put on.

"Do we have to go away" wails Brenda

"Yes we do" says Ruby, herself putting her own coat on. The little group are accompanied to the station by Tom.

"Now here's a thing" he thinks to himself "it was me that was leaving last time"

People climb aboard the train and Ruby sticks her head out of the window.

"Don't worry about me; it's you I worry about"

"I'll be alright, just make sure the girls are looked after" says Tom

"Don't fret; we'll be at Peggy's. We'll be fine"

"Oh" he says "I nearly forgot"

He put his hand inside his coat pocket and pulls out a tin of peaches, Ruby's face lights up.

"Where did you get that?" she asks

"Mister French saved it for me" he beams

The whistle blows and the train starts to puff its way out of the station.

"Bye daddy" shouts Brenda

"Bye daddy" comes a little voice from Frances

Tom watches as the three faces disappear into the steam. He feels empty as he stands there on the station.

"There's no use worrying about it" he says to himself and he walks off.

Back home, Tom sits in his chair with his newspaper, he looks around him but all he can hear is the clock on the mantelpiece ticking. But apart from that, the place is quiet, No children running around playing. He enjoyed seeing the girls happy at play; he thinks to himself that it will be very quiet for a while.

"I hope the war doesn't last much longer" he finally says

Nothing.

"I hope this damn war finishes soon" he says a little louder

Suddenly, he realises Ruby has gone too.

"I miss the children" he says quietly to himself.

He rustles his newspaper, and then drops it on the floor.

The quiet, the hypnotic ticking of the clock, the weariness of the war, all sends Tom to sleep. He is back in No Man's land and standing there with his uniform on and gas mask. It is misty all around but he can see close to him but the mist obscures vision more than two metres away. It is quiet, very quiet except he can hear his heavy breathing and he is warm inside his mask. All around him swirls a green mist while off in the distance a bell rings briefly. In the mist he can see a shadowy figure, and out steps Cecil. He has no mask on and his face is blotchy red. Several huge blisters are on his face and neck, his jacket is undone and his shirt torn and grubby. In the holes Tom can see more red blotches.

"Tom, why did you let me die?"

The boy holds out his hands.

"Why Tom? You let me die"

Tom pulls off his mask.

"I didn't, I was out there myself. I was gassed just as you were"

"But you left me in No Man's land. You left me there, Tom"

More blisters appear on the boy's hands and face.

"I'm only seventeen, and you left me there"

"Cecil"

"See, you can't even get my name right, it's Cedric"

"Cedric, I was out there too. I was in No Man's land too"

"But you let them gas me!"

"I had no control over the war"

"You left me to die"

Cecil stretches his hands out further and makes a step towards Tom.

"You didn't look after me, I trusted you. You left me to die"

"No, not this time" Tom says and with that he wakes up.

He is panting and sweating, he grips tightly onto the arms of his chair. He turns to look at the clock, it still ticks away.

"It's just a dream" he says to himself "just a dream"

He releases his grip and relaxes his whole body.

"Yes, it was just a dream. I had nothing to do with the outcome of the war. It was nothing to do with me"

He stands up.

"Sorry Cecil...er, Cedric, but I have to help myself. I'm off down the pub"

He put his jacket on and starts to walk out. He stops, turns,

"I mustn't forget my glass"

He picks up his pint glass and walks out with it, scarcity of materials means that punters often have to bring their own glasses.

1945

The news has reached everyone who go absolutely crazy with joy, the war has ended and Tom has now been through two of them. He is standing on Marylebone station while he holds up the letter that told him that Ruby and the girls are coming home. The train pulls in, steam fills the station. People get off; he looks up and down the platform. He looks towards the steam engine then hears "Daddy!"

Turning to look there is Brenda running up the platform towards him, she throws herself at Tom.

"Daddy" she cries

She is followed by Frances who also launches herself at Tom.

"Daddy" she cries. Tom picks her up and holds her.

"We missed you Daddy" says little Frances.

"I've missed you too" says Tom. His eyes then focus on the figure who stands behind Brenda.

"Ruby" he says "welcome home"

"Tom" she throws her arms around his neck.

All the way home, the girls recount their stories of their time in Bristol.

The whole street has children returning home and the parents lay on a huge street party. The table runs the length of Portnall Road; flags have been stretched between the houses along the length of the street. There are jellies and chocolate cake; most don't know where all this food came from nor do they care. Pop for the children, something a bit more substantial for the adults. Frances picks up a Union Jack on a stick from somewhere and is waving it about while Tom laughs at her.

"Well, this is it, I hope" says Tom

"What do you mean?" asks Ruby

"The end of the war. I hope there will never be another one; I don't think I could cope"

Ruby hugs Tom.

The sun is going down and the street lights come on, the children stand in wonderment at these lights, some being too young to remember seeing them before the war. A big "oooh" goes up as the lights come on. A bit more singing before the children are tired out from their fun, and are taken indoors leaving the adults to clear up the mess. The girls have been put to bed as Ruby slumps into the armchair in the kitchen; the Union Jack is limp against the far wall.

"If you're going to stay in my armchair then I'm going down the pub" says Tom.

"You go ahead, I'm going to stay here" she says

"You'll be alright, yes?"

"Yes, I'll be fine. You go down the pub"

He walks down to the Falcon and thinks the old pub hasn't really changed over the years. Alright, it's got electric lights now but the character is still there. He walks in, the air is electric, there is a band playing tonight. Four chaps, banjo, trombone double bass and drums.

"What's this?" he says to himself

The band finish their number and the crowd slowly calm down. One by one, people notice Tom is at the door as they turn to look at him. When he coughs, the whole pub hears him through the silence. They part to form a channel which leads directly to the piano. He walks slowly past the faces, every now and then; someone would raise a glass to Tom. He sees his three old friends Ralph, Lionel and Vernon, who are now very old indeed. They are a reminder that they survived while many of his other friends didn't. Apart from Bill who is standing in the crowd and raises his glass to Tom. He gets to the piano, sits down and lifts the lid. He sits quietly just for a moment to remember the war he fought in, the war where he lost so many friends, in fact, many people lost many friends. Many soldiers who'd survived Passchendaele have deep resentment at those who planned the battles, the memories stuck with them forever. Many soldiers still have bad dreams about the battle many years on; they had become insular and suppress their memories of the war, and sometimes wouldn't talk about it, like Tom. He would always have his bad dreams although his ability to cope with them is getting better. The people at the top who took their countries to war were stupid. He was proud he did his bit for the country but can't help wondering what was it all for, what had, if anything, been achieved? He looks around at the happy but worn out faces all looking at him. He wonders why he was still here, but quickly dismisses the question because he is grateful that he is still here. He lasted a lot longer than the six months the doctor told him, and he has a happy family. Suddenly, a pint of beer makes a thud on top of the piano; he turns and looks at it.

"Hey!" he grabs it and takes a sup then places it back on the top.

"Right then..." he says and immediately rams his fingers down on the ivories to start the first tune, the other musicians recognise the tune and join in. People join in with singing. Tom thinks this could be the start of a new band and turns to look at the other musicians who nod in approval. He turns round to see the happy faces of the people in the crowd, they are enjoying themselves with smiles on their faces but the biggest smile is his.

EPILOGUE

TOM MAY HAVE BEEN LUCKY enough to have survived the war but it didn't do his musical career much good. He didn't become the superstar of the day because as is with all music styles, they get superseded by another musical style. The Music Hall fizzled out before the end of the twenties by which time, Tom couldn't get a band together. However, he was a legend in his area, all pub goers in the area (and some of the other adjacent areas) knew of Tom and his piano playing abilities. He never stopped doing the thing he loved most, that is playing the piano. He occasionally turned to newer styles but still carried on with what he loved, and what the pub going public liked. Every night was a party night.

The Great War took a lot away from a lot of people, for some the ultimate sacrifice of giving up their lives. Those that survived had the job of rebuilding their lives from where they left off, often a difficult task. The war had changed them both physically and mentally; the stress was so great that it aged them beyond their years. As for Tom, he nearly paid with his life but he survived, and rebuilt his life. He didn't give up despite the many losses in his life.

Tom survived both wars and lived to he was eighty years old, when he died in 1970. Although this novel is fiction, the family characters were real (although the characters outside of the family were made up). Tom is my Grandfather and his second wife my Grandmother. The story is centred around the dates discovered in my family history tracing, along with family stories, the events leading up to these dates had to be surmised. It is known that he was a postman, he went to war and was gassed. I felt he lived a life that was full and so I had to tell his story.

Lightning Source UK Ltd.
Milton Keynes UK
UKOW02f2009260515

252314UK00001B/8/P